Which Way to Nonna's House?

Which Way to Nonna's House?

Second Movement of the New York
Novella Quartet of the Four Seasons

Joseph Nicolello

RESOURCE *Publications* · Eugene, Oregon

WHICH WAY TO NONNA'S HOUSE?
Second Movement of the New York Novella Quartet of the Four Seasons

Resource Publications
An Imprint of Wipf and Stock Publishers
199 W. 8th Ave., Suite 3
Eugene, OR 97401

www.wipfandstock.com

PAPERBACK ISBN: 978-1-6667-5674-6
HARDCOVER ISBN: 978-1-6667-5675-3
EBOOK ISBN: 978-1-6667-5676-0

12/06/22

"This episode will have lived for years in his memory and even in his wonder; it had the quality that fortune distils in a single drop at a time—the quality that lubricates many ensuing frictions."

—HENRY JAMES, "The Lesson of the Master"

". . . what is the position of the saint in a world teeming with the most complicated, the most sophisticated forms of evil?"

—THOMAS MOLNAR, *Georges Bernanos: His Political Thought and Prophecy*

I.

THIS IS A TALE of beginnings and epiphanies, written in a moment whose darkness would appear to render such a testament irrelevant. But it is the very assumptive nature by which the prevailing western narrative has rendered untold persons mentally enslaved to cultures of envy and hatred, whereby it is a disruption of this corporate-revolutionary stalemate in which literature, or poetry, might flourish. In essence, we have been molded as a society of exteriors rather than depths. We see, for instance, that today we are wont to think that certain persons ever suffered, that another type inflicted suffering; that a faulty premise of one country in history ever partaking in slavery has aimed at the mental and spiritual death of the masses through the simulation of an excoriating majority; which is ironic, as these claims are often made by persons in Nike shoes, typed through their iPhone, both the products of present-day slavery. But what is irony, then? Irony is found at the cost of a sacrificed understanding of how things come into being. There where slavery is the norm, it is normalized by the beneficiaries of its recipients. If one wants to know, then, how and why men owned and own slaves, consider the psychological impossibility that would occur in suggesting that today's anti-slavery chanters do away with their Nike shoes and iPhones. Therefore in a century the ones who long to break statues today will themselves be memorially despised by their generational descendants, who with the sloth-gift of posterity will rage against what is obvious only after the fact. For ideological thinking has a built-in timer, a clock that is wired by destruction; it is predicated upon a lack of unbiased historical knowledge, and has its flames fanned by disposable propagandists. The opposite, then, of ideological thinking—or brainwash—must be something more in line with the natural law, with which this novella, among other things, is concerned.

And the natural law, rather than the stupidity of hatred, was certainly on the side of the men and women who left their uninhabitable Italian lands in order to make for themselves a new life here in America, often willing to go anywhere, but finding work in New York City. This is such a case, a novelistic snapshot: but before we meet Giuseppe, Nonna, and some others along Arthur Avenue, let us take a moment to consider the spirit that was with the women and men who made this part of town their own, whose best parts are the fruits of their labor, and whose lesser parts are of an inferior, alien culture. Thus the predominant dialogue of permanent information would have us believe that all legitimate hope was lost; and meanwhile around every corner miracles transpired, communities came together, and history and identity were reconsidered by those men and women rightly, furiously skeptical of the prevailing nature, whose objective is divisional bondage; let literature, then, work toward the opposite, as did our city's builders.

For those men set out on the gilded path prepared by that most glorious man, Christopher Columbus, some in order to obtain funds with which to return home, others to stay put in the New Land. There were women, too, though the men greatly outnumbered them as Italian emigrants for whom a sea voyage—imperceptible by today's technological standards in its time-shattering, claustrophobic filth—was less hazardous to body and mind than to stay put in the ravaged, exploited lands of home.

Some, in the mid-to-late-nineteenth-century, sold flowers and fruit, with no guaranteed intimate spiritual direction to help guide them through such inglorious set ups; though the Faith had been dealt a blow back home, here it was even worse: one priest for every eight thousand Catholics. At each of the eight legitimate churches at the time of Nonna's earliest mythological forerunners one was further bulwarked by that odious American invention of pew-renting. Not only did a man put his life on the line crossing the vast ocean, but he might have done it all just to sell apples and geraniums on some insane street corner, without even the luxury of Mass or spiritual guidance. But this, Nonna always reminded them, was just one little puzzle piece among so many.

Tolerating the Irish and the German, other workers were selected for more dangerous work, such as bridge-building. These men had themselves an irony thrust upon them, in the form of manufactured light: digging the bridge foundations at night was a job lit by calcium lamps otherwise used for stage productions or political rallies, here shone down upon emigrants, breaking their way through traprock and basalt at fewer than six inches per week. Of course, methods arose by which to blast their collective ways to twelve, eighteen inches down per week, and with such maneuvers came a horrific spike in equally horrific deaths. Those who did not die underwent what Nonna called "the bends," with blood randomly bleeding from orifices, working around the clock, caked subterranean blood strewn with evaporated visual memories of nitrogen bubbles.

A world with neither smart phone nor air conditioning!

Boats from Naples, immigrants from southern Italy single men, Catholic, rural—they came from desolate valleys of isolation, mountain-chains dividing them from the mezzogiorno, a geographical fragment abandoned by technological feudalism . . . indeed there was a time when Giuseppe's father, Giuseppe Sr., had heard that a nice Italian film was playing in Manhattan, shot on-site in Italy about the lives of simple folks . . . but the film made her weep, truly weep in a way that was itself mythical. The film was *Tree of Wooden Clogs* . . . the left-behinds, with wooden plow, perhaps the most severely illiterate people in all of Europe before taking by the thousands to sail played the musical chimes of freedom, flashing within the despairing minds of men—as the industrial revolution transformed the interior and exterior of land and man alike, elsewhere, these men and women remained to perimeters defined by an ability to retain the sound of their church bell; to go beyond the realm of being able to hear it was as imperceptible as crossing the Atlantic had been in earlier days. Unbearable outside events pushed them, along with a host of Jews, to finally relocate, a testament immortalized upon the little ramp that leads up to the door of Teitel Brothers.

Their great privilege was to be considered equivalent to African barbarians, both persons sentenced to the lingering death of geographical destitution; these illiterate left-behinds had seen the gates of purgatory, considered just as colonially expendable, less whole persons than statistics in the midst of colonial plundering, enslaved by their supposed own in an ongoing fashion around the globe that seems to have been purposefully forgotten for the sake of keeping its advocates out of the spotlight.

The average person had eleven dollars in his pocket when he arrived, and eventually made his way to the padroni. Mines, agricultural jobs, railroad work and construction sites were other jobs available.

Beggars cannot choose, but those men avoided factories if they could. Giuseppe's father, something of a cinematic connoisseur, understood this when he had seen a long, lesser-known film entitled *The Human Condition*; its ending was the logical terminus for factory working in the great chain of being.

Docks, roads, aqueducts, building sites, and rapid transit lines were much more preferable. For men less enthusiastic, or able, to throw themselves into such potentially lethal predicaments of backbreaking labor, one by about 1900 might find himself work as barber, establishing a system of fruit vending rather than selling loose pieces alone.

For the children there was opportunity for money as well, perhaps working as an organ grinder or bootblack. Little Giuseppe had himself insisted he be able to earn some money as a bootblack, having heard about the job one day at lunch, and having shined his friends' shoes for quarters at school. Despite the elder Giuseppe's insistence that his son cherish his youth and accept a weekly allowance that would bring in more than bootblacking, the boy would not let it go until he at last the day came when his father let him set up shop in Grand Central, watching at a distance. The little boy's first customer was a morbidly obese homeless man, who smelled of cheap gin and worse, and asked the boy if he could have his shoes shined on credit, to pay him back next month. Looking down, little Giuseppe saw a grotesque, scabbed potato of a toe, with yellow curling nail and lined with dirt, waving hello from a shoe that looked as though it had been chewed apart by a rottweiler and cast into a garbage dump. Thus Giuseppe learned that even the life of a bootblack was difficult, and resumed putting his energies toward study, and helping mama wash dishes in the evening.

Italian women found the factory life less annihilating, and chose two pleasant types in particular: tobacco factories and candy factories. Nonna had herself once worked in a candy factory for a day: "At lunch the girls told me I needed to read the *Communist Manifesto*. I didn't know what the hell that was all about and told them there was only book I needed to read, besides maybe St. Theresa of Avila or Brother Lawrence once in a while, which my late brother—God bless his soul—Antony, the librarian and later monk, gave to me. But these girls wouldn't stop. So I read a few pages of that crap and decided whoever wrote it was an idiot, from a family of idiots, by and for idiots all over the world. Reprobates, really. So I quit the job that night and had a big beautiful family, blessed by the Lord. To that end I thank the candy factory girls, doomed as they were; they helped me witness what I had only until then heard was evil stupidity actually take a look for myself."

They saved pennies and helped bring over willing relatives, family members, siblings; the worst New York had to offer was still a step up from the hopeless misery of home. The worst off would themselves be redeemed, those godly men who alongside the Irish sold rags, bones, and cans to junk dealers; those men had the spirit of Christ in them whether they knew it or not, as their chain of actions would testify, culminating in Mt. Carmel.

Where Nonna grew up, out on Mulberry Street, it cost twelve dollars a month for a three-room apartment, which in turn housed sixteen: mama and papa, numerous sons and daughters, and lodgers fresh off the boat looking for a sober place to sleep, pray, and prepare for the revolution of each morning. The Hamilton Ferry took them to family members out in Red Hook, and they also visited the Navy Yard and Greenpoint once.

When Nonna's forebearers had their homes and lives established to a point of being able to make a next move, be it returning to Italy or living in a more idyllic apartment, they looked north rather than across any of bodies of water. True, it was less cramped up north, where Harlem is today; but it came at the price of putrid air derived of gasworks, stockyards, tar and garbage dumps.

And as a preface to that beautiful church in Belmont, Our Lady of Mt. Carmel, came first one in East Harlem, build by the hands of these same men. Thus a pair of accusations, as vermin are forever hounding after lions—that they were pagans! But what could one expect from the distant, if lesser known glorious man, of Marsilio Ficino, and his doctrine of platonic theology? These men were no pagans, nor idolaters, but cherished their home sanctuaries and private prayer; dogma and the public both had periodical ways of exhausting themselves, and man was perpetually forced to turn inward, from Athens and Jerusalem into next year. But then accusations spread that these men were so busy building churches they were seldom in others come Sunday! But did not the Lord say, "The Kingdom of God is in you?" These were Nonna's favorite words; and her way of life proved this to Giuseppe not by any particular act or deed, nor by the way that she carried or presented herself, but by the very fact of her existence. One with the most ardent complaints could not have a cup of tea with Nonna without leaving angry that one had ever been so hard on oneself; for here was a woman with one lung, who'd met grand-pappy as the sole survivors of a tuberculosis ward; such was their benevolent privilege, agony, poverty, and the permanent shadow of death.

There was even an old Italian edition of Carlo Collodi's *Pinocchio* inside Nonna's secret drawer, the one in which she had halfjokingly said once that there was also a revolver, and holy water, should any demonic looters that summer pay her a visit, and profanely disrupt her cappuccino and precious box of rainbow cookies.

For once upon a time, in a fractured land, there was . . .

"A revolution!" cry the children of all ages.

No, children, once again you are wrong. Once upon a time there was papa again looking desperately around for any type of work, and a big stick of pepperoni.

Then it was the crack of dawn and little Giuseppe pretended he was sleeping when mama came in to awaken him, that joyous, mysterious scent of coffee brewing, papa gauging the morning temperature out on the fire escape, a quick breakfast then the three off, en route to Arthur Ave.

For all their relative poverty, the Pacelli tribe made every effort to keep alive a legitimate spark of holiness in their little lives. Giuseppe Pacelli came from a rough, large family—all workers for the city, he, his father, and four older brothers, from the pits of manholes to the tops of skyscrapers—of seven, uneducated in nothing outside of agrarian hardship until about ten years ago, when his second-eldest brother graduated high school. What could be swept out of understanding as sheer ignorance and hardship had, however, a philosophy of its own: that God was both incomprehensible and the only thing worth fixing one's heart and mind toward, and that God's Son was Christ, and that the Holy Spirit rounded out the Triune God, to whom there was no other path outside the Catholic Church. That this position appears intolerant today is not a matter of bigotry but of an actual belief in the creed; it is a statement on our place in Gomorrah to the second power, within which there remain, nonetheless, treasures hidden in darkness.

Such a treasure was for Joseph and Mary Pacelli their boy, Giuseppe. Theirs was a love at first sight amplified by the series of agonies that immediately followed their wedding. After her second miscarriage, Mary was shaken in both mind and act. She took three part-time jobs in a row to supplement her husband's income as first a limousine driver, and then a cabbie, tending bar a couple of times a year around the holidays. Each of these jobs led to a panic attacks which increased in severity while coming faster each time still: at Barnes and Noble she lasted two weeks; at the supermarket, she lasted one week; then at the hot dog stand in Grand Central terminal, she lasted fifteen minutes.

At this time, the Pacelli family and her own fragmented tribe, scattered across New York State, made the peculiarly collective decision of terminating all contact with Mr. and Mrs. Pacelli. Mary had been a black sheep of the family following her own mother's death from suicide when she was all but seven; she despised the new woman her father married, and graduated high school only by his determination to pay off the school with lump sums from his new wife's stately income as an heiress of a tobacco enterprise.

Following the third breakdown, Mary spent time in a psychiatric institution, albeit less than two weeks. It was deemed the tragedy and stress, coupled with abrupt alienation from all the family she had left, or had obtained through her marriage, was enough to drive any sensitive person temporarily insane. She was given a mild sedative to help her sleep, which did not alter her mind, and which she was never compelled to take at any time other than when she was tired in bed, after having said her prayers.

Still, the stigma of having broken down and gone to a hospital was itself all the proof those around her needed. In fact, it did not matter that she was neither insane, nor needed affection more than ever; like one rendered guilty by way of accusation, such was the fate of Mrs. Pacelli, barren, scarred, given on occasion to crying in church alone, and beside her husband, having no one in the world to confide in but Christ and the Blessed Virgin.

Mr. Pacelli was torn. But he was torn in the sense that a man who is serious about his vows is torn. That is, his heart broke to watch his lovely suffer this way, while never breaking in a way that lent itself to the prospect of abandonment. Instead, he was paralyzed at times with the sickness of a childless life, flailing job prospects, and a developing sense of alienation from his own brothers and father, based on monetary inferences. He could not comprehend how his brothers and father could have thrown him down into the well like this, because he was more after God than he was that symbolic pathology of money. Increasingly he saw himself in the role of one with a whip, driving out money changers, or arriving on some fateful evening with a sword. None stood by him amidst his stretch of darkness in the noon blaze of existential reconsiderations save his mother, or Nonna, whom we shall meet shortly.

Now Giuseppe Sr. did not actually envy the things that his brothers did together with his father, in the same way that Mary did not mind her family falling away from her; the absence stung sharper than what was in fact absent. He did not care for live music, sports, famous restaurants, or ski resorts. He was a Solomonic medievalist: everything was vanity. But it did bother him that it all had proceeded without any conversation or even, one might say, a trial; that when he would go to visit his mother with Mary up at Arthur Avenue he only did so when she was there alone, and that there were updates from his brothers and his father by way of the photographs upon the mantelpiece, and all the pictures magnetized to the refrigerator. They were indeed traveling the world together, selling a contemptuous mix of insurance, hardware, work-gear, clothing, and audiobook sets that won awards, on how one can start a business and rise to the top faster than any other method out there: for the sons of immigrants, by the sons of immigrants. Meanwhile, Giuseppe Sr. took less shifts at the cab, drank a little more than usual, and prayed with Mary that her next doctor's appointment would bring good news, that a better job would be given him, despite his reputation now established as black sheep of this particular Pacelli clan; in short, a miracle, or an image of God's justness.

Can it be said that Giuseppe Sr.'s brothers and father drew the wrath of God based on their treatment of their son and brother? And can it be said that Mr. and Mrs. Pacelli were unflinchingly chaste in that desert of trembling and pain that was the timespan from her second miscarriage into the third attack, entering thus the breakdown and its aftermath, the present moment?

It was right around the time that school begins in some places, the first week of September, when Mary felt there was a little glow, or presence, inside of her. On the one hand, she thought, this could be either imaginary or hunger; on the other, it could be the divine spark of life. Whatever it was she would find out soon and knew that her jaw hurt a little bit from smiling throughout that morning more than she had smiled in the past fifteen months. She was able to see the doctor the following Tuesday, the 11th, which was nice.

As for the men of good fortune, Nonna had mentioned to Giuseppe Sr. that the business had taken off so well at this point that the five of them had been invited to a breakfast at the World Trade Center; it was at this point that Giuseppe Sr. knew that now a financial distance had passed between them that truly rendered him a familial serf. But that was only one, ungodly, way of looking at it. Was a man bad because he lacked the desire to grow rich? The best men the Bible had to offer did not seem bent, let alone pathologically obsessed, with riches; quite the contrary. And yet as he stepped out of the doctor's waiting room that morning, his faith lilted; he had the gospels on his side, and yet the world—as symbolized by his father and brothers—had irreversibly rejected him. Now their business, his own opinion of its futility be damned, seemed destined to become an officially internationally traded corporation. But he did not know what Nonna knew: that the brothers and the father had poured all their collective savings into the movements that culminated in this moment, the morning of this, their crowning appointment. For a day or days, meager Joe Pacelli, as some of his acquaintances called him, had more than his betrayers, in that his admittedly pitiful bank account was in fact stable, and not in the negative, nor up in the air.

He was buying two iced coffees from the cigars and magazine shop when a madman came bursting in; Joe's immediate thought was that the man was being chased by his potential executioner. Likewise, the cashier took the pistol beneath his countertop within his hand.

"Turn! Turn it on! Turn it on—this is war!"

Then the man, clad in neon work vest, muddy boots, and filthy denim pants, punched on the TV himself, making it wobble.

There were those two iconic buildings on fire, it seemed, with much more happening, and more to come.

As for Mary, her face was like a reviving flower when she got the news: her doctor had told her it would be impossible to conceive. And here she was, to the contrary.

She was like a rainbow when she spoke of the boy during the pregnancy. When he was born in perfect health and she had rested long and good, she thereafter moved about with the weightless, prayerful grace of an angel. A veil of the soul had been removed in the shadow of national and familial sorrows beyond dreams; and for Joseph Pacelli he was no longer a pharaonic slave, bound in solemn grief to Job's daughter. Now he was simultaneously the widow's son and the father of a miraculous little boy born out of the ashes of cataclysmic terror and betrayal.

For six years Nonna was held afloat by various charities, social security, and the crumbs of her threefold family. The calls, emails, acts of generosity decreased. Prices rose. Nonna had never even graduated the tenth grade. She was banking on her husband and sons taking care of her for life.

How could it be then that she radiated holiness, both in-person and in memories of encounters with her?

This was something Joseph, Mary, and even little Giuseppe in his own way were thinking of on the highway, making the drive up to Arthur Avenue, the former once more going to yet another job interview, Mary redolently faithful albeit anxious—

And as for Giuseppe, he was thinking of rainbow cookies.

Passing Rodham University and getting closer to Nonna's apartment, to the mystical Arthur Ave., Giuseppe's reflexive mind fluttered with images. Even outside of Nonna, her apartment and her presence, the neighborhood itself seemed like an extension of her soul. There in the trees, in the eyes of little cats peeking out of boxes, the scent of freshly baked bread in the air, and roaring swirl of an espresso machine. All of his aunt's warm, marvelous insights that were known the block over, notions plucked right out of mid-air, mid-conversation, melded together in a way whereby the street became synonymous with the person. Thus the little boy secretly bit his nails behind the cover of a comic book, and anticipated the nearing, familiar flashing signs for the zoo, the baseball stadium, the university, daydreaming of proximity to mythos.

Such was his state of mind when his mama turned around from the passenger seat to whisper imitatively:

"You see, Giuseppe, how some streets have ca-ca and garbage all over them? Flies, dung, filth?"

"Yes, Nonna," peeped his father, his eyes flashing in the mirror.

"That's how you can tell where the Italians don't live. And that's also what the future of this country will look like. Maybe you'll end up back in Italy after all."

"I can row boats in Venice," said the diver to little Giuseppe, "Like Uncle Mario did when he was a boy."

"But then Uncle Mario put his ridiculous paddles down and went to the University of Rome and made a fortune afterwards. As long as you do that, I'll let you row boats till your arms go from pink to blue."

Then his dreams turned into reality as they found a parking spot right out front of Gino's on the first try.

"This is a good omen," Giuseppe's parents agreed. "A very good omen."

Up the old, warped steps, fresh garlic and sauce in the air!

Giuseppe's papa tiptoed up to the door adorned with its sparse cross made of twigs and an invisible dab of super glue that Giuseppe had made before the Christmas holiday of pre-K.

"Quiet, quiet," whispered Giuseppe the Elder.

He tiptoed to the door, Giuseppe guided likewise by his mother's soft hand.

"Now you know what to do Giuseppe . . . walk right up to Nonna and giver her a great big kiss!"

Giuseppe had momentarily reflected on this manner for the better part of the morning, in between bursts of hairspray: he in general disliked kissing relatives except for his mama, and then there was a cousin who was old, somewhere up around fifteen, who Giuseppe admittedly found gorgeous, perhaps the girl that would come to mind if one were to ask him, "Who is the prettiest girl in the world?"—and even then, however, he was terrified to kiss her hello.

To that end he was absolved, though, by Giuseppe the Elder having overturned the tables at a somewhat recent family gathering, after hearing his cousin's father had said terrible things about Giuseppe's papa behind his back . . . Giuseppe was inside washing his face and immediately whisked away from that wild party, but it is rumored that Giuseppe's father even smashed a piggy bank and loosed his sister-in-law's caged bird!

But it was not a problem to kiss Nonna.

He knew today would be special in that Nonna was not in her famous chair. After all she had been through in her life, the toil and the sacrifice, her big cushiony chair seemed like a perfect overture to paradise.

"Hello! Aw!" cried Nonna, scooting down to meet Giuseppe's cheek, and vice-versa.

"Her breath is never stinky!" Giuseppe realized. "And her little plain apartment here never smelled like old peoples' homes like the others I know, like my friends' grandparents and even when someone passes me sometimes in the store, I think, 'That's the smell—it smells like an old attic.'"

Giuseppe twiddled his thumbs, glancing about for a dish of rainbow cake or bowl of candies. Perhaps Nonna was waiting until mama and papa went out for the day?

"What do you have planned for the day?" smiled Giuseppe the Elder's lovely wife.

"Oh I think we'll see how hot it gets. But the main thing is just to be here, right Giuseppe? Nonna misses you!"

"I miss you too, Nonna," the boy blushed, spinning on his heels to feign the appearance of studying the calendar of the saints. "I got first place in art and poetry, and daddy and I said maybe Nonna can tell me some stories I can use for my masterpieces!"

Giuseppe's papa crouched down to him and gave him a loving kiss. The faintest prickle of stubble burned him, coupled with a scent of expensive birthday cologne. But the general household stress of recent weeks seemed to have dissolved in the brief glance papa gave Giuseppe in returning to his full height; as Nonna and mama discussed for a moment some mysterious womanly things, a bit of the pain of seeing his father so upset with being fired again from work, thereafter even drinking late at night, once caught weeping—O, how it was so unlike him. And Giuseppe knew he should not have even witnessed this, save for the little hole in his bedroom door that he peered through at night on the troubling occasion his parents were whispering, visibly wracked with anxiety, into the wee hours.

But a true sense of relief rushed through him then having seen the look in his father's eyes, the boy standing there beneath Reubens' calendrically-abridged portrait of Augustine.

Then in a haze of hugs and kisses mama's keys were twinkling round her soft finger and the door they had just walked through was closing with click behind them.

Nonna stood at the stove, looking down at her old kettle.

"Should I have another café, Giuseppe?"

"Mama and papa say that three cups is good for the day."

"Well, don't tell mama and papa, but I have more than that. But eh, maybe I should relax. How about I rest my eyes for a bit, and then you can tell me all about school and your awards when I come back out?"

"Sure."

Like clockwork, Nonna retired into a most comfortable position, one whereby she would "rest her eyes." Giuseppe listened for her fan to click on, counted to one hundred, and then tiptoed over to the Hershey's tin over the breadbox. But there was nothing inside except some stamps, a thumbtack, rubber bands, and a supermarket coupon.

Then Giuseppe recalled the last time he was over, when Nonna was reading Pinocchio to him in her recliner. There was a slim drawer attached to the nightstand that he recalled Nonna putting some pocket change into. He wondered if that was change for homeless people; maybe.

He tiptoed into the living room and sat down in the enormous chair. For a moment he closed his eyes and would not open them; Jesus, though bound by frames and a barrier of glass, was looking at the boy. He said to him, "You have just got money for your Holy Communion; why are you not happy with this? Think of all the Peanut Chews you can buy with ten dollars. Refrain, Giuseppe, and open not that drawer."

But then the boy realized that in fact no one was speaking. Silence reigned; how can one be thinking words and hearing and seeing them in absolute silence? Confused, and against the Lord, he lightly tugged on the nightstand drawer. Behold! A five-dollar bill!

The door clicked closed behind him. He heard a chorus of voices and light music coming from both east and west. But to the left, about half a block down flew what appeared the Italian flag, the sight of which, met with the recaptured possibility of someone from Nonna's building catching Giuseppe outside, caused him to put out his little left hand, thumb extended downward in order to make an L; the opposite direction of the thumb was in fact left; this he had learned at recess. If he knew anything, as he made it out of sight of Nonna's building, it was that he was going left.

Where blew a flag, alas, was but a red, white, and green emblazoned corners store as seen through the wavering rays of amplifying humidity. Beside it stood something of a makeshift, gated-up bicycle shop, closed for the weekend. He crossed the street.

On the other side of the street were a row of stores that, to his mind, lacked the flavor of what he knew and cherished on Arthur Avenue. There was a mattress store, real estate, taxes, investments, a barbershop, nail salon, and an Italian tailor who also sold imported garbs. The sight of all those suits in the window reminded him of Communion—then he was thinking of mama, with her hairspray, and how she forced him to part his hair to the side! But the girls did smile at him that day, when he was injured and insulted by having that necktie choke his little neck, spray that made his dirty blonde hair crisply noxious, and all the rest of it. Why did men grow up and wear suits like this? he pondered.

As he window-shopped this array of torture devices, he felt in his pocket for the ten dollars: it was there. Also there, as he took a step back, was Nonna's apartment building in the shop window's reflection before him. Then he looked down, squatted, and looked upon his little rippling face in a puddle.

But then he was thrown off guard by a wailing ambulance going off behind him—he extended his little hand again and inverted the signal, in order to steer clear of Nonna's building entrance; he went the way of his thumb, rather than against it.

Now at this street corner he was suddenly at Arthur Avenue. Men with suspenders and cigars in their mouths were moving barricades into the crosswalk, establishing piazza. The little street was basked in a perfect shade of old, towering trees, protecting the row of multicolored storefronts from an abrasive sun. The bank, too, he recognized, in that there was always a downturned milk crate beside the free newspaper stand of weathered yellow plastic. Little Giuseppe was tempted to climb atop the crate to get a view of his recently lost tooth, up in the winding mirror-wall by which he knew now where he was (in one sense). Yet a strange sense of self-consciousness came upon him, suddenly out there in the world all by himself: he knew for the first time in his life how little he was out in the world, now with neither papa, mama, nor Nonna beside him, and that his occasional habit of trying out new ridiculous faces in mirrors or reflective pools, which would then be employed in the classroom for his friends' great benefit, was something childish, and that being out in the city alone was the opposite of childish. Looking around at what appeared to him a sort of parade at sidewalk's end, it seemed best, even if it meant his adventure was thwarted, and thus his mission to have a slice of rainbow cookie cake, was in vain; now it was more important to get back into the apartment, where Nonna was still sleeping.

As the little crosswalk man turned neon white, Giuseppe looked back once; in a flash he saw an old storefront with discolored newspapers serving as windshields, where he could have sworn Nonna lived, near the café and pastry shop. He did not recall aged newspapers in any windows, and was nearly run over by a screen-staring wobbling mob of tourists, when he crossed over, went limbo under the police barricade, and entered into the piazza proper.

Now he realized that in knowing he had entered the piazza, that he had no idea which way to turn for Nonna's house.

An elderly woman with sandwiches bags of bread pieces sightlessly cast bread pieces about the perimeter. The turning body, with its scent of neglected basement, delivered a shadow all across Giuseppe's line of sight. He ceased squinting through unshaded concrete, and beheld a terrible noise that followed the winding shadow: she was feeding the pigeons.

Giuseppe turned from the woman to the open street. There before sat a very old girl, at least sixteen, with long brown hair, fare skin, and a cloud-white dress.

"Hi," she said.

"Hi," imitated Giuseppe.

"Is there any reason you're staring at me?"

"Yes," Giuseppe peeped.

She tucked her phone into the leather purse.

"Well?"

"I'm looking for Nonna's house," said Giuseppe.

"Um—what?"

"I made my Communion and got money for savings. Papa gave me ten dollars to have dessert this afternoon with Nonna."

"You're all dirty and sweaty," said the girl. "Come here."

Giuseppe reluctantly allowed himself to have dirt rubbed off, his hair parted, and sweat dried by a set of napkins the old girl had pocketed, for reasons unbeknownst to her, upon leaving Dominic's earlier in the day.

"Well, you look better now. Where is Nonna's house?"

"That's what I want to know," said Giuseppe. He felt the crowd of people accumulating around him, though—thankfully—none seemed to be paying attention to his encounter with this stranger who may as well been his older sister.

"I don't understand how you got down here all by yourself. But my name is Aurora, and I can help you before I meet back up with my parents to drive back home in a little while."

"I remember! It's by Tino's."

Aurora smiled.

"Well, then it's just back across the street that way."

She pointed, and the pair looked backwards toward the start of Arthur Avenue. Giuseppe knew that this was not the way; but then he considered that he had been wrong thus far, and perhaps with some luck was wrong now.

Then his thinking was cut off all at once by his guide taking his little hand in his. This sent shockwaves into his head. He had only ever held the hand of mama or Nonna before, and even during the Christmas Eve play at school the priest had had to explain to the youths that it was no sin for Mary and Joseph to hold hands in the manger, even though the children were actors playing them, and as human beings, holding hands like adults do who must be in love, that dangerous state of mind that the priests and nuns avoided, that Jesus himself took no part in, and which Giuseppe had hitherto assumed was something, like the dishes, he only did with his mama when either no one was looking or when she, like Aurora now, was guiding him across a busy street. Thus he squirmed through the maze of café scenes, flavored smoke and a tint of spirits, blue flames glowing in the dark of cupped hands, and the clanging of pots, pans, cups, and silverware in the Luna restaurant beyond.

"You know it's Tino's, because there's Padre Pio! And look at the statues and artwork inside!"

Giuseppe looked, his lips zipped shut; it was a beautiful place, but one he had never seen. He was positive Nonna did not leave here and told his confidante as much.

"But this is Tino's."

"I think I messed the names up."

"Well if this isn't it, you can come to the market with me," said Aurora. "But you need to hurry up! Let's go fast!"

The pair galloped ahead.

"My parents are picking me up because my boyfriend and me broke up today and he left me here all alone. Let's go to DeLillo's first!"

"I'm sorry to hear that," said little Giuseppe. "A real man like me would never do you any harm."

"What? What do you know about being a man, or harm? How old are you?"

"I'm seven," said Giuseppe.

"Oh my goodness," smiled Aurora. "You are really a crazy kid. Do you want to hear what happened with me and my ex-boyfriend?"

"Not in particularly," shrugged Giuseppe.

"He owed my dad thirty dollars. My dad gave him thirty dollars for gas on a trip we took to Syracuse, because he was visiting a college there."

"Thirty dollars is a lot of money."

"No it isn't."

"Yes it is—I could buy a big box of Lincoln Logs with that and still have money left over for a holographic Derek Jeter."

"Logs? Holograms? Well, maybe you can call me in eleven years when you're eighteen."

"That's a long time from now. How long is that?"

"Eleven years. Hold on—my mom is calling me."

Giuseppe took a seat on a little water spout, sized just right, and wiped the sweat from his forehead and arms. All around him were groups of people talking, singing, laughing, some even dancing. It dawned on him again to look out for landmarks that might lead him to Nonna's. Yes, he would be in for a mild beating when all of this was said and done. But for now he thought about those action movies he heard about when people get some money, end up in a situation that is bad and time is running out, and someone says what his father said sometimes: "Let the games begin!" To this end he thought first of cappuccino chip gelato with ice cold water, filtered like mama made it, with no ca-ca floating around in it. He could also smell pizza and envisioned a slice that was twice the size of his head. Yes, he salivated, I want the ice first, then the pizza.

I, Giuseppe, would never be allowed to eat in that order, but I need to find out where they sell cappuccino chip.

II.

MEANWHILE OVER ACROSS THE street at Rodham University the Graduate Committee for English was just concluding its preliminary approvals of prospective acceptances for doctoral study when one of the deans arrived. This dean was called Dr. Coonskin, historian of twentieth-century America and apostle to the poetical blend of graduates; her abrupt presence, swiftly breaking up what had been for Prof. Mly, head of the department, the nearly initial seconds of a horrific silence, lent divine credence to the latter's secular mind: it appeared help was on the way in a matter concerning the preservation or annihilation of a reputation, and no option in between.

What had happened was that once again one of the professors had made an email account and sent out a series of blackout-drunk confessional emails. This could have been, in theory, someone from another department who had simply compiled a list of English faculty and staff emails. However, some of the references to ongoing projects, affairs, disputes, were those of the sort that not even everyone in the department knew about. Such a strange, painful outburst could have connoted the spouse or friend of an English department member; but then the emails were so eloquently written, including footnotes and a rhetorical grammar veering toward fascism in their eloquent perfection.

This email, like the rest, took a full ten minutes to read. It concerned an inexplicable series of gambling tales, a narrative concerning the loss of increasingly large amounts of money at casinos, online poker, sports gambling apps, and references to shady Bronx basement groups of various card games. Whereby the idea was that the author of these desperate emails was Barry Mly came about, in that two Christmas parties ago Prof. Mly had arrived in bad shape, having started drinking, in her words, "Not at the bar or at home before the party, but three years ago . . . I've had a drink in hand for three years straight . . . because my husband is gambling all of our money away, and I cannot stop him;" so it was concluded among the department members who read the emails that this was at least someone with some connection to English, as the cc'd parties were always exclusively English faculty and, again, the discreet bits of knowledge being lamented made it impossible to realistically consider anyone else authoring them.

Worst of all concerning this latest letter was a clue that had slipped out the night prior, concerning what the anonymous author referred to as "gentrifier's guilt," a sort of suicidal remorse over having dispossessed communities in order to secure her million-dollar apartment in the heart of Harlem. Mly was ferociously vocal whenever a given news station used any given phone-caught flash of racialized violence around the city with blacks getting the short hand of the stick. She was pathologically silent when her own were raped, mugged, butchered, and beaten; but such was par for the course of tenure. Despite this, even the most self-hating of the roundtable found her—if it was indeed her—transcending the bounds of sense in her confessional emails. Even the Israeli-American professor Moshe Silverman was thinking of incorporating the emails as literary texts in his most popular seminar, "Towards a Holocaust of Whiteness."

Barry Mly was taken from her dread, however, of part insomnia and part wine headache, by the appearance of the dean, who might have some news on a most serious matter.

Dean Coonskin, all ninety pounds of her, was flustered; her skin was a color that called to mind more than simply being indoors too much, but almost as though she had a sort of inverted tanning booth, or a tanning booth reversed, and was ghostlike in her plain black outfit, exclamatory red lipstick and black powder around her wide, dark eyes, straggly graying hair, and black boots which seemed to suggest a willingness to re-arrive at some of the more raucous nocturnal orgies of her gothic youth.

The exasperated dean held her phone out before the perplexed roundtable of charlatans, as if for all to somehow see from variegated distances, although her screen had automatically turned black.

"Hold on—everything—I mean everyone, resume, I'll be right back," said Prof. Barry Mly, chair of the department. Prof. Mly was not unlike a strange cross between the fairy and the giraffe; she was in the process of moving from the churning out of pornographic fantasy novels into the sphere of, what at least the department perceived of as, revolutionary politics.

Mly knew Dean Coonskin well and had at first found her relatively recent dissertation topic distasteful. But now every news outlet in the western world was advocating for racial justice by reexamining the recent past, and thus Mly was quick to change her tone.

Thus when the dean appeared like something out of a dream concerning a bender and a burning house, Prof. Mly gleamed at the prospect of confiding in the distraught dean, and perhaps helping her, thereby gaining points of her own.

"It's Mother McShane," panted Dean Coonskin.

Prof. Mly said, "Dean—Dean—relax, please, it's OK, whatever it is. We were just wrapping up our working waitlist for autumn."

"Oh, jolly! So you," outreaching her pretty index finger, erect and buoying, resuming, "It's maybe not that big a deal then. Mother McShane thought—I thought—there has been an incident, but OK, now I see it's not even a big deal here. I was scared, though."

Prof. Mly looked at the poor dean, pondering if she always went a little cross-eyed in times of great upheaval. The former swallowed something rancid, last hour's pint of wine. She eyed the adjacent room, her office, which in truth contained a clichéd bookshelf of popular racially abundant swindlers. Beneath it, however, was her stash of wine.

She said, "Here, let me see your phone. Now I have a good ten minutes—let's go into my office."

The wiry pair pranced past the island table without chairs and its unkempt contents: the latest MLA, vegan granola bars, and a draft of a referendum on censoring a recent graduate of the program, who had written a Swiftian work most critical of the program. That, the last two uneven slices of what resembled carrot cake, a single Rodham University napkin, curled at the edge, and a fly.

"I can't believe they still don't do anything about the flies," said the dean worriedly.

"The janitors are slow, but that just means we must be patient," smiled Prof. Mly, locking the door behind her.

She sat down across from the dean at the weirdly small table.

Dean Coonskin asked, "Is this, like, a children's table?"

"I don't know, really. It was a gift from someone in the neighborhood."

"And the windows are still boarded up."

The pair observed the pair of windows covered by corkboards nailed to the wall.

"Some of the students are afraid of heights. We do not want to be disclosive."

Dean Coonskin smiled plainly, thinking, "Did she mean 'uninclusive?'"

"But before anything!" The chair of the department leapt up, bent down and unlocked the wine cabinet. She poured two dixie cups of red. Noticing the dean enter, via thumbs, into rapid-fire at her phone, the chair of the department downed both cups, placed two sticks of cinnamon gum into her wide mouth, and refilled the cups, returning.

"Alright Dean Coonskin, lay it on me!"

"I got your email about the alumnus and his book. I am yet to read it myself. But that is not the only reason I'm here."

"It will be most helpful just to collect your thoughts on legal proceedings, dean. Even your initial impressions."

The dean lengthily, nasally exhaled; then she scratched her hand for a moment.

"My concern is one that is . . . well . . . historical. In essence, won't bringing the person—or bringing legal proceedings against the person, bring him publicity that he does not deserve? I mean I had never even heard of this person as an author, which is kind of my point. Also, I did know him and spoke to him a handful of times, and he struck me as . . . well; he struck me as genuine. I don't know how else to say it. He does not seem stupid or malicious, which was the impression I got from you, Prof. Mly."

"But! But there is a big difference between a person and their work, you know. The person is all public, with the secret curtailed for the sake of moving ahead. The author, however, is all private, and only comes up for air to let oneself be known."

"Are you absolutely positive that this is slander, though?"

"He attended this school, and there is a school in his book."

Now that she was saying it aloud, even over the warmth of the wine aglow within her, her case seemed much more artificial than it had last night, when she sent out the mass emails.

"Alright," sneezed Dean Coonskin, "We're going to need to isolate at least two passages and, but—but before we like do that, I need you to be more specific about what's going on. Your email was very emotional, Prof. Mly, but there was nothing actually specific in it. We—Mother McShane and I—gather the impression that you were exceedingly hurt by something in this book, but in all five pages of your letter you never once mention the actual despicable passages. In truth, you mostly just attacked the alumnus with derogatory language, berating them, him, as it were.

Prof. Mly shed a small smile, listening to the meeting adjourn next door. In a sense the department chair was on the cusp of being terrified: this was the source of the silence in her morning's meeting. There was no way anyone did not see the email: but their wooden cheer and total silence on the matter, which was earlier perplexing, now made perfect sense: Prof. Mly was on the way to becoming the caricature of the alcoholic, though no one dared say anything out of the fear of being fired.

"Barry, I think that Fath- excuse me, I mean Mother Mc-Shane made a good point when I saw them earlier. They said that among other things, from their understanding of the committee's looking at the book, that one of the satirical parts—"

"This is much more serious than *satire*! Dean—how dare you!"

"Barry, please—just hear us, me out. They were concerned that one of the more invigorating passages concerns, in the book, Banned Books Week. Banned Books Week is next week and we always have a spread out down at 2Pac Library. We might want to wait until it's over, wait ten days is all."

Prof. Mly thought this over. A part of her, when she was younger, would have concurred that this was a good idea on a sound blend of constitutional and aesthetic principles. At the same time, the young woman who would have concurred such would have never have been lambasted in print by a former student. Then, to make matters worse, there was nothing so concrete as actually having Mly's name in that part of the book, Rodham University did not exist in the temple of the text, and even a reference to one Don Insect in the text, when in "real life" there was a Tom Aphid, was still not enough to successfully sue the author in court.

"I want to add, Prof. Mly, that this might also be very unfruitful from the economical point of view. From what I recall of the author he lives in extreme circumstances, at the edge of the streets, and abhors materiality. I mean, I guess we could sue a man who has no money . . . but what if he just continued to live this life of notorious simplicity, bordering on the ascetic, and he never even obtains a well-paying job with which to incrementally pay you for the damages occurred through his poetry?"

"Poetry! That's a laugh!"

"You might laugh, but really, this is the strongest reaction I have ever seen elicited from any student or alumnus project on campus. We need to also consider the fact that he may have planned this all in advance, and that his next book entails an aging professor who takes a young author to court during Banned Books Week, or tries to strip him of his degrees in among other subjects literature, thereby placing in the company of other writers who have been brought to court based on their books. Some such authors, I have noted, include Flaubert and Joyce. He was about as stout as Flaubert the last time I saw him, and perhaps as, at the core of it, as sick in the head as Joyce . . . so listen, Barry, my friend, I really just do not want you getting hurt. We might be in deep here, but please, I am praying night and day, let us not overreact."

Barry Mly took another drink, leant up across the vertical corkboard, for a moment hallucinating an below, and an ameliorative street comprised thereby.

The dean was disturbed at Prof. Mly's drinking. It cut at the heart of her thesis, that absolute power corrupts absolutely. Were Mly less rich, she would have been fired for drinking around the clock. The situation really made Dean Coonskin want revisit Plato's first dialogue, *Euthyphro*, as there were ways in that short, neglected text that Socrates framed things that the dean really felt kind of joyously gnawing at her breast.

However, there was nothing Dean Coonskin could do if she did not want to lose the job that it had taken her twelve years straight of graduate education to obtain; she did not realize that at the heart of this there was its own sort of Socratic answer that, alas, the kingdom of heaven was perhaps an old tub, a bottle of hemlock, and friendly yapping dog.

"Mother McShane, ever since they became Mother instead of Father, has been on a mission, the mission of justice. We want to go with Mother on that mission."

"Where is he—I'm, no, sorry, I mean she?"

"Please be mindful not to let slip that hateful rhetoric," Prof. Mly said icily. There was a dab of wine on her shirt, slowly expanding. "Mother is doing Story Time at the nursery."

"We—have a nursery?"

The dean was confused.

"Mother McShane opened a nursery after there was a spike in undergraduates having children. In our mission to end oppression, we began recruiting more students from the Bronx and the rougher parts of the city instead of all over the world . . . and such people have many children. Mother McShane's work is courageous. She is even—don't tell anyone—planning an all-nude week on campus, so that, Mother says, we can go back to our first parents, Adam and Eve. Everybody naked for a week—it will good for the children says Mother McShane, in celebration of Genesis!"

Dean Coonskin bit her nail. It seemed that something had gone horribly wrong. No. Horribly wrong was about three decades ago. Now was something different.

The dean was suddenly interested in finding out more about this author that Mother McShane and Barry Mly hated so much. All she knew was that he worked under a massive, framed painting of Goya.

Maybe she could find out more about him from the librarians, with whom he must have been acquainted.

"We'll do dinner this evening with Mother, and discuss how we shall proceed. Thank you so much, seriously, Dean Coonskin."

"Yes, Barry; I think we will do a great work together."

The dean was off to find out more about the renegade poet before dinner with Barry Mly and Mother McShane.

It did not take long, seeing as the poet had worked for a short spell in the library before being relieved from his duties in what was a harsh series of words one of the librarians had overheard in the lobby of Rodham's 2Pac Library:

"As you may or may not know, I identify as—well, you know, never mind," bellowed the stout librarian. "To the point, yes, when Hamlet was working here at 2Pac I did not know him well, but overheard him in conversation in the lobby with another graduate student, where I really wished he would have been joking."

Dean Coonskin procured her tablet, a little plastic sort of tubular rod, briskly making note of the bandage at the librarian's left temple.

"When I got there, the student was worked up and telling Hamlet he, the latter, had offended him. I can ask the student if he would like to talk to you about it. But Hamlet responded to this visibly upset student, saying, 'In what will be the first and last time I ever reference that little weasel called Shapiro, facts, sir, do not care about your feelings. I would have cited Virgil or Horace were I not seconds away from stepping into this elevator.' The student then said, 'Hamlet, truly, I actually like Ben Shapiro. Maybe I really did misunderstand you. Why do you not like Shapiro?' Then Hamlet, acknowledging the little circular lightbulb bell of the elevator, said, stepping to the extending doors, 'The truth shall make you free.' At that point he walked in, his back to us, and must have pressed the [><] (making a hand gesture to indicate in-turned arrows), for he was gone. Then I fainted, and that is how I got this cut on my head."

Mother McShane and Professor Mly walked sulkily through blazing heat, across a discolored lawn, and to a bench within tranquilizing shade.

"We must clamp down on emails, Mother. Is there any way we can have hardware installed into the computer systems in order to monitor emails before they are sent? Or to, say, freeze the emails of terrorists and insurrectionists who write these hideous things, then paste all of our emails in, and send it out? Could we not at the very least hunt down this person, or people, with their IP address?"

"I wish it were so simple," lisped Mother McShane, whistling at a pair of distant squirrels. "I might be able to bring it up later, in fact you should come."

"Go where? I'll do anything to put an end to Hamlet Hamlet Hamlet Donatello."

"At six o'clock there is the annual Ignatian Transgender Pastoral Installation in Manhattan. This year will have twice as many speakers and panelists, as last year's was canceled due to the mostly peaceful protests that destroyed part of what was Keats Hall, now Sanger Hall. There will be a short film screening by a most cherished alumna, called "Concentration Camps and the Problem of Whiteness," followed by a one-act play by a local playwright and racial justice activist, entitled "Toward a Holocaust of Whiteness." They are supposed to very funny, from what I understand. Anyhow, professor, if you come with me, I will ensure your issue is given adequate attention. Will you meet me at the President's House at 5:15 pm, and then we can attend these events together, thereafter bringing this cyber terrorism issue to the fore?"

"Yes! Without question! Only, Mother, I do have one—very quick, too—question. Just one, quickly, then I'll go."

"Yes child, do tell?"

"Mother, if I spend two million dollars on an apartment in Harlem, but only donated ten dollars to out anti-racist pedagogy forum, and just fifteen dollars to Black Lives Matter, will God still love me? The apartment was very expensive and if I could go back in time, I would donate my millions to causes of racial justice, and with ten or fifteen dollars attempt to live inside of a cardboard box on the Bowery, in repentance for the sin of whiteness, the history of slavery, and other things that make me cry."

"My dear child," whispered Mother McShane, consoling the weary professor with a palm upon her shoulder, "You are not alone in this fight for justice . . . these were the exact issues a group of us discussed at a recent Drag Queen Story Time out on Long Island . . . I think you just need to get more active, is all, and remember that God loves you."

III.

Looking up, Giuseppe did not see Aurora, neither nearby nor distant, before or behind, or down either side of the shady street. He walked ahead through the piazza, parting the sea of persons, and turned left to step into what appeared a religious gift shop with maroon awning.

Giuseppe was relieved that the man and woman talking at the cashier did not immediately ask him where his mama was. So this is what it feels like, I see to, to go out and about alone. There was a gelato cooler near the entrance; but he was not tall enough to look inside.

Instead he set his sights on a colorful array of imported pastas, types familiar and others rather unfamiliar, in both name and size. Here too was the type of oregano that Nonna used, that came not pre-crushed but as a plant that one broke apart in one's hands at the counter. There was also a fine array of oils, sun-dried tomatoes and peppers, and materials for making coffee.

Camouflaged by the stand of pastas, little Giuseppe was able to move away from the foodstuff and into the part of the shop that offered the religious wares advertised in the window. Here was a beautiful little wooden figure of St. Joseph that one could set up in one's home to protect one's family from havoc. And besides St. Joseph a porcelain figure of the Blessed Virgin, whose quality and shape lent itself to a light touch, as foreseen by the little inscription at Mary's foot: DO NOT TOUCH! ASK FOR ASSISTANCE! There are many rules one must follow in the real world; so many signs and notices, symbols and devices! A beautifully illustrated Easter book had a display copy available for glossing; little Giuseppe could tell by a light smudge of fingertip only visible at a specific angle, and if one was barely foot feet up from the ground. But as he took in his hands the illustrated book, he found himself absorbed not by the words accompanying the various biblical scenes, but the conversation transpiring behind him, in a blend of broken English interspliced with Italian, and the end of a classical album that had been playing engaging the front of the store with sudden silence.

"I tell ya, the Bronx Zoo will change a man. How, why, when, I dunno, but the zoo in Bronx can change a man."

"That so?"

"A woman, too. A woman it could change, maybe a man, too. What time is it? Oh I got five minutes. But I tell you, no kidding, staring at the rhinoceros when its horn hits the black gate bar, bending over to unload, dis kid came up to me, woikin d' as a summa gig, I guess. The kid recognize me from Rodham; I taught the kid how to read poetry it seems. So now dis kid, wit a handful of rhino crap in his hand in a plastic bagg, says, *Long day, says the rhino's eyes, filled with the casket flash of cameras.* Foreign languages, whistling a tune, my granddaughter's hand leaves mine she laughs so hard."

"The poor kid musta bin mawtified."

"So I tell 'im, I says thanks, Pindar, for your choral song. Now we keep going on, me and the little one, and all a sudden a monkey's in a suit banging on a tambourine. Me and the kid laugh, me in dis navy-blue suit, she in skipping around, just like her mommy did. She laughs so hard she cannot look at me, and this poet kid is walkin around again, reciting *does not notice the rare October sun, which today, who knows why, is coming down infernally.* So I'm sunburnt like at the beach, dinosaur excrement and crazy poets, a squealing grandkid, watching the lions pace the cracked clay ground. My granddaughter sneaks the cotton candy from my bag, and hides a piece in her miniature purse."

"Aren't they sneaky?"

"We hold hands again, and walk toward the aquarium. "Grandpa, how did they get a whale in the thing?' I could only smile, smile only, and tell her it is a mystery, in the tone of voice which implies the mystery is one I may or may not have something to do with. We stop at the restroom, soda fountain, the photobooths, and scratch at our lime-green paper bracelets. The second grade, I marvel, wiping sweat from my brow. Diane shakes off the photo-sheet like a Polaroid, scans the evidence, and laughs hysterically. I kneel down, and she draped my arm across my shoulder. There she is, shot by shot, smiling, bunny ears, squinting, Frankenstein. And old me, bearded, tongue out, scratching my armpits, kissing Diane on the cheek. "What about the sting ray," she says, "How the sting ray go into the thing without stinging everybody? Was the sting ray on Noah's Ark, granddaddy? granddaddy?' But then she dragg'n me to d' falcon. First the falcon, then the group of Bronx schoolchildren scabbed, screaming and cursing in line for hot dogs. Why do hotdogs taste good only at a barbeque with friends, or alone, in the city?"

"That's true."

"Den she says 'How come people work at the zoo?' Her hand is a third the size of mine, I remember and watch her little girl's purse sway to and fro in the sunlight. Parakeets scare d' shit outta me. 'Don't you think it'd be fun to work at the zoo?' I ask, 'It could be a whole lot of fun to work at the zoo!'"

"I don't think you'd be very thrilled if your granddaughter was working at the zoo."

"As long as she don't act like something that belongs in the zoo I don't care what she does. So I says, 'But don't you want to be a doctor a lawyer instead of working at the zoo?' And den she says home come people are janitors? Why don't they go to college?' 'Everyone is different, Diane, I says to the kid, not everyone goes to college. I know plenty of good people without college degrees. I know plenty of good janitors, and even more good people who work in manholes and dive bars.' 'That's silly!' 'Why is it silly?' We stop and observe the aquatic guide inscribed within the air-conditioned hallway. A fine watercolor maze of sea-life masquerades around the velvet roped-windings down. There is a dimming of the lights. The counter-woman gives Diane a lollipop. 'What do you say?' 'Thank you!'"

"Uh huh. Say, is that a little kid behind the aisle there?"

A pair of professors entered, shushing one another, tiptoeing toward the elderly speaker.

"Anyone New York can people-watch," whispered Prof. Joyner, "But really, if one is going to work in the arts, one must learn to people-*listen*."

Giuseppe noticed the polish of their shoes. It shone like sunlight in a fractal movement of a car doorhandle.

"—walk ahead through the dimmed aquarium entranceway and taste the cold air. I wipe sweat out of my beard, and daydream of our wondrous evening ahead at Peter Luger's Steakhouse. I saved my whole bonus for that. Working the phones at the Verizon building by the Seaport might not be where the money is, but it's where I am. And here I am, and here is my daughter, again taking my hand in the October Sunday early-afternoon. 'Granddaddy,' Diane says, looking to her light-up sneakers, 'Who do you know who works at the zoo?' 'I know the whale,' I say, 'And the monkey, and the tortoise, and the penguin, and even the rhinoceros.' 'I liked the rhino,' said my granddaughter."

Giuseppe had been listening to all of this with great intrigue. It reminded him in a sense of when he had to read but was thinking of something else, that he could be looking at something right before his eyes without seeing it. For a moment he had been at the zoo; but now a trail of blackberry brandy barely concealed by cigarettes and a stick of gum awoke from his reverie, hand-carved mahogany figurines of the Holy Family in his little hands.

Then he turned around and looked up at the woman, who herself had a suspicious smile, hands on knees and a peach-colored top that smelt fragrantly of intoxicating perfume.

"You're a little young to be out by yourself, aren't you?"

"Nonna took a nap so I came out to find rainbow cookies."

"How about the girl you were with? Is that your girlfriend, sweetie?"

"She said we were going to Tino's but then I realized that Tino's was the place I wasn't looking for. Which way, please, to Nonna's house?"

"I tink d' guys next store might help 'im. Go t' Mario's—day been dare a hunnid yeas. They know da wuttayacawlit—day prolly know 'is grandma."

Giuseppe was entranced by the voice, one that he had never heard out in public like this before. He had thought it something of a localized anomaly, at occasional family get-togethers, where the singular Italian-New York accent flourished without restraint. How different was it from the other voices he heard! Did all of the older men speak this way on Arthur Avenue? What strange lives they lived, talking about crazy things transpiring at the zoo!

Whatever it was that held him so enraptured, the voice coupled with a golden crucifix indicated to Giuseppe that he was on the right track to returning to Nonna's house very soon. It was a good thing that people knew her here, and seemed to want to help the little boy rather than take him straight home, tell on him, and get him in big trouble.

"Da wuttayacawlit," he giggled to himself, accepting a little piece of candy and a kiss on the forehead. "Da peep-o here—they are so nice!"

The shop door fell open, and Giuseppe was recaptured by the droning chorus of a thousand feasting voices.

IV.

Out on her little fire escape haven above Morrone's Café, waving hello to the kindly freemasons over at Ivana's Pizza, Juliette lit a cigarette of success, having for the first time in her life had the nerve to call off work from her father's seafood restaurant. Her boyfriend, Patrick, was very stoned; one's eyes burned just looking at his thin figure, adorned with a basketball jersey, khaki pants, boat shoes, and a Columbia University cap that had for all the weeks they had been together irked Juliette. For having taken one course at Columbia, three summers past, she felt it wrong to give off the impression that he, her boyfriend, belonged in any sense to the famed university.

But Patrick was the first boy to ever tell her she was beautiful, which was a stretch, albeit one made relatively authentic in the former's familial catholicity. And as Juliette looked both twenty and forty-six at the same time due harsh pockmarks across her face, noticeably bitten-down nails, and a strange clown-like laugh that reeked of middle-aged divorcees in bars packed with derelicts rendered acceptable by the blinding clouds of mentholated cigarette smoke, she was forever drawing attention to all three of her worst features at once: the extreme, spontaneous laughter made her slap cupped hands to her mouths; and the hands were terribly mangled, almost a prelude to some orphic rite, or dreams of child Dionysius's toys; and when the clasped hands fell away from her painful face, one was left with the crossword puzzles of pockmarks momentarily thrown into pale relief by touch, before automatically

35

reverting into a harsh, terrible red that one could not say was un-noticeable or incidental and tell the truth.

Except for Patrick Luciano, who had his own catch: the most bizarre stories in the world, fueled by drug-addled memories of drug-addled events that may or may not have taken place.

Now they were out on the fire escape. Juliette was in her anx-ious heart ready to drag Patrick to church, in order to pray the rosary so that her sin of having lied to her father would not run absolute roughshod over her now theoretically free day, which she could feel at once was in fact—like all sin—its own type of hideous bondage. But it was just at that point that Patrick stamped out his cigarillo and recited his dream:

"Having taken the plane to Saturn, Juliette, my greatest fear was the moment of contact with other lifeforms: the moment, mind you, and not the form or the thereafter itself. My theory, as I spent months researching everything from propaganda to its opposite concerning the new space planes and developing voyages to other hitherto mysterious planets, was that what awaited me was in any case nothing like what we had seen in alien documentaries, films, and TV shows. This weird, chance formulaic was itself grounded empirically: in my life I have found that a thing, be it bad or good, is not what one envisions the thing to be. This seems to work in the abstract, as in something like mammal-popularity, or fame, or an incoming president, or feedback on an assignment. Really, the list is endless, though it might also include online dating, reading a classic work, or moving to a new city: the thing that all of this has in common is that the pre-experiential mind conjures whatever it can concerning that which it has not experienced, and thus en-gages in extensive fantasy—pure fantasy—on the way to the thing-itself. So even in the case that there were aliens that looked exactly like they did in that one movie: still I could not take comfort in ap-proaching them, for the concept of my mind rendered unto actual aliens had in essence nothing whatsoever in common with a film, despite the film's potential similarities to the horrifying mutation of eternal stupidity and violence we call "reality.""

"I was told the flight could take up to eight years and packed accordingly. I had with me one hundred volumes I planned to read or reread, and a decade's supply of morphine. My theory was that Saturn would have better tools available to help one ween off a decade-long hallucinatory coma of numbness divided by warmth.

"However, as the plane ship took off, I found myself unable to read or inject anything. There was the massive box of Dailies (pills that constitute a framework of eighteen hundred, mostly healthy, calories), three feet high, six feet long, three feet wide, cushioned interior."

"This is so weird," hawed Juliette.

"I do not recall the world shrinking to the size of a pin before vanishing, the way one might a balloon released into the air. In fact it did not feel like a decade passed, and I did not feel much wiser, despite the hundred books rearranged, some with pencils and multicolored neon stickers emerging outward , and the Dailies about three quarters gone. In truth, I was skeptical at first; if it were not for the face that all those Dailies were gone, and the books so obviously read, I would have been terrifyingly offended."

"Then Marlon Zink and Tiny Moa entered the ship and released me from the incubational bed."

"They looked exactly the same expect perhaps for makeup designed to make them appear a little older, and some artificial white in either's hair; the latter was obvious to me, because I once decided to go back on a choice to dye my hair; too little of the stuff made parts of one's hair too artificially gray by contrast with the untouched parts. And yet I wanted to look younger, they, to my knowledge, older. Ten years older. There was something counter-clocklike about it all, but I had no time to inquire.

"We are officially not on Earth anymore, my friend."

"What's it like out there?"

"Digital Colonists have been busy making a place that looks hellishly like home. Not just the home of Earth, but particularly America."

"Dear heavens; why?"

"Oh jolly—as if I know!"

"There are apparently monks here, which is why we're waiting. They're ferocious in their proselytizing all over again, now that we are on a planet that is virtually untouched. They crucified a man who said that the Roman Catholic Church was simply a real estate company. Then they tortured another man who said that no institution is anything more than incidental to the Holy Spirit, whilst the majority are detrimental."

"I don't want to hear about the torture," I said. "How in tarnation are they preaching their doctrine here? Why? Have they actually convinced people that part of Jesus's plan, through Rome, was to colonize Mars? This should be the end of eschatological practice, rather than the relocation of the End Days. Are there any other religions here?"

"The usual suspects."

"I felt sick hearing this.

"Then I vomited into the waste basket beside me until I was out of breath with tears flowing my burnt eyes.

"You need to think of it this way," said Tiny, "That if you don't sign up for at least one of them, they're all going to try and get you. There are already rumors of a Uranus Savings Bank and a sort of digital currency. The idea is holographic cash. Without any sort of political-religious alignment you'll be unable to buy or sell, let alone move freely."

"There are metallic dogs around, and scorpions, and one needs defend oneself."

"One oughtn't fear the future; to fear it is to have no idea what the future actually is."

Juliette watched the light foot traffic below. She embraced the scarce breeze coming in, perhaps one of the few on what would be a sweltering day.

"I don't get the part about you referring to the usual suspects."

"Really? That's the part of the dream that struck you?"

Juliette refolded her legs. She picked at a clean nail. She thought it would have been better to have just gone to work today. Then Patrick's hand grazed her elbow; she would in fact go to work today.

Outside the street was packed. Now people had to turn sideways and tilt their bags certain ways in order to zig-zag through the piazza without spilling their or another's drink.

The shop owner again bent down to smile at Giuseppe, this time giving him a scoop of cappuccino chip for his travels. Now the man who had been telling the story from out of sight appeared—he was an enormous man, both vertically and horizontally, and the veins that bulged through his hands through a forest of white and black hairs, wrapped around the cardboard rivulets of brown paper bags of hand-rolled cigars, made Giuseppe's eyes bulge open.

"Come on, kid. We'll go see Mario and help you get back to Nonna."

"Mm hm," nodded Giuseppe.

"Where ya parents? You all live with Nonna?"

"No, we live by Clinton Street in Lower East Side."

"That's way down!"

"Mommy and daddy had a café but it closed. Now daddy is looking for a new job today."

"What happened wit d' café? What was it called?"

The big man had stopped out front of the green store on the corner. Giuseppe could not hear what he was saying to the man pointing to and explaining all the multicolored cannisters of imported oils.

"Sorry kid, I hadda see sumtin."

Little Giuseppe squished the paper bowl into a sharp-edged oval, and took it down like he had seen others take liquids down on the shaded table of an approaching drink stand.

"Was d' ice good?"

"Ice?"

"D' whattayacawlit; da gelato ting."

"She gave me cappuccino chip! Cappuccino chip is my favorite! And mommy's!"

They stepped into Mario's, where Giuseppe tried to look around for something familiar, but was visually barricaded by the zoo man, waiters, a busser, and forthcoming, someone the boy could only guess was Mario himself.

"Ay kid! You lost? Come on, hop up." He scooped him up and into a bar chair. Giuseppe had never been on so high a seat before; and instantaneously he even had a shot glass full of unshelled pistachios and a glass of coke with ice cubes and cherry before him, as the alternating fan breezed on fresh air in waves.

As Giuseppe stumbled through the maze of walkers, he came upon a sparkling cerulean milk crate. Its cleanliness caught his eye and kept it. For some reason lingering crates were almost exclusively pigeon-colored, pigeon-stained, or kicked in; but there beside the sleek black nylon tarp of the piazza dining vestibule, strewn as it was with violet-red cursive lettering, the boy tested out the crate by leaning into, looked both ways, turned it over, and took a seat.

It was five Mississippi-seconds before a boy cradling a cardboard box, whose makeshift roof was flopping up and down, approached him.

"Say—you like cats?"

"Cats? Like the animal, the pet cats?"

"Yeah."

"No. Just dogs. But not all dogs. Just the good ones."

"How about kittens? You like kittens, right?"

"Kittens ain't cats."

"But let's say you got a kitten, even when it grows up, you always remember the baby face and see it forever. My priest said that cats and dogs are like our little siblings in the animal kingdom."

"A sibling? What are you talking about?"

The boy held open the lid and knelt down. Giuseppe looked in; half a dozen tiny little kitten faces were looking up at him, some reaching, all meowing.

"They are cute!"

"I'll sell you one for a quarter."

"I don't have a quarter."

"What about fifty cents?"

"I can't buy a kitten and then my parents don't want it—then what?"

"You can hide it."

"Then it would die," Giuseppe said. "How come you have a box of them anyway?"

"Out in my Nonna's backyard there's some cats she always took care of. But now they know that Nonna gives the best food and milk and the cats all started to live in her backyard. I got a rock, bunch of rocks, though, and chased the ugly fat ones away. From up on the roof we threw down buckets of water on the ugly black ones. So then the pretty cats stayed and had even more than are in this box, so I decided to try and sell some today. Nonna said that cats don't remember things like we do and these little guys just want a home, end of story."

"Maybe go to Christopher Columbus Park and ask some old ladies there if they want them."

"How come you're sitting on a crate out front of my uncle's restaurant?"

"I'm taking a break," said Giuseppe.

"From what?"

"I'm trying to find my Nonna's house."

"House? Where does she live?"

"If I knew that I wouldn't be looking for it!"

There was the entranceway to the market—that looked familiar with its several doors, and commotion of people coming in and out, weaving between the ice scooper on one hand and the cigar roller on the other. Giuseppe inhaled the delirious scent of sprawled tobacco leaves; then a wave of bags was coming toward his head, and he looked up beyond the ice scooper and set his eyes upon a black cloth square, with red and green writing, and a bright pink cartoon pig seated contentedly therein. He recognized that cartoon pig from somewhere—Nonna's refrigerator? He bolted up, zigzagging through some stationary tourists, and hooked left through the fractal space of a closing heavy glass door.

He looked up with shock into what appeared to him some type of alien hovercraft that he had seen watching *Unsolved Mysteries* late at night (or had once tried to, before being scared to death and never even looking at the specific channel on TV) and he sneakily went through channels on the rare occasion his father ran out to the store and his mother fell asleep particularly early.

A wizened older gentleman reached up to the hallucinatory chandelier, plucked a piece of pepperoni, and took it to the cutter. Giuseppe watched the big metal machine go back and forth, walking sideways alongside the long glass display case to the table with a spread of cheese cubes and unpitted olives.

"Do you like spicy, kid?"

"A little bit," said Giuseppe. "Not too spicy."

"Then you'll like this. Here."

Giuseppe accepted a little black plate of cheese and pepperoni, the combination of which melted in his mouth. Then a hand, from some body cloaked by myriad passersby, was extended his way, offering a piece of Italian bread dabbed with olive oil, and a small cup of black cherry coca cola, held up and cooled to perfection by a pair of ice cubes.

Having finished his plate, Giuseppe looked up again at the alien artifact of the magical chandelier; it reminded him of a cartoon he had seen where real people were zapped into miniatures, and became the size of one's hand. He could see a group of such people perhaps finding a new civilization in a pepperoni hovercraft, and that the pork store may very well have been the gateway to another cosmos.

Or as with broccoli being little trees of an imaginative forest, this pork above was a civilization reversed all to itself, full of hidden treasures and adventures.

A waft of delicious pipe smoke came in through the held-open door, where a voice not unlike Nonna's snapped him out of his dream.

The feast was still in full swing. Only now he had to wash his face and relieve himself, surrounded by giants who took turns stepping over and around him, the pork chandelier receding into a glorious distance; for now he was propelled to turn at once, spotting an opening in the sea of bodies, and driven as if magnetically to the open market door. He recalled from many Friday afternoon lunches with Nonna that Mike's Deli has a bathroom, and that the lunge upstairs to it might further help burn off some of the weight of all the food satisfactorily sifting in his little frame.

There were the cigar-rollers at work, laughing and singing in the cavernous horizon of concrete floor and wooden ledge, booths and cutters, moving fans blowing lightly, and noises breaking from the adjacent miniature café, with all its open spread of cannoli, cake, and cookies, maroon, vanilla, chocolate, mint-green, cake-yellow, golden.

He skipped over a little puddle near the bar, the deli-front, and streamers from some concluded party, en route to the tall doors that took one to the bathroom stairs.

As the proximity drove waves of pain through his frame, Giuseppe realized that no one here had ever seen him without Nonna. And further still, his stomach felt like a beach ball; should he consume another pinch of anything at all, he might pop.

Thus he wove through the long line, up to the bathroom, and out, hiding beyond a row of backup chairs, waiting for a moment to run back down unrecognized, and listening:

"Upstairs it's OK. PG-rated. Little nephews and nieces layin' around the TV. We had some presidential candidates here last week. This week we got a man start over bologna. I never seen a man get taken out on a stretcher because of bologna."

Giuseppe looked up mystified, surrounded by loosely familiar voices, great mysterious wooden barrels, and a pair of men rolling in kegs of beer somewhere beyond Mike's.

"Ay—would you like to try our homemade wine?"

"Where's your husband, Mary?"

"Downstairs hangin out wit summa da guys."

"Heh, figured; I tell you if a man getting shot over anything it might as well be speck. I knew a man that lived on cannoli for every meal. He lived to be a hundred and one."

"He's enjoyin imself. If he's not drinkin he's a neurotic mess that geezer. It should be his birthday every daya the week. If I could afford it I'd do it. I'm worried. He hates his job. Now he start fights over bologna. He losin' his touch."

"Tellim he awta start eatin' cannoli ina morning."

"I think he too late for cannoli to solve his issues. Sad, really; I fear for the future of this country. I'm with him there. Nope, no

booze for me this month. But ay, He's convinced the USA is leaning towards fascism, that this news industry is a loada shit, that
we're all brainwashed, everyone except him. He go around thinkin'
everyone in the world wrong except him."

"Wow."

"Yeah."

"Howda you put up wit 'at?"

"I tell him I have headaches. I tell him I'm goin to the library.
That typea shit. Then I go to bars, clubs, anything decent, where
they aint talking about human nature eternity et cetera."

"Divorce don't run in his family and I don't have the energy
to cause a riot. I go where all that meaningless shit don't matter,
that's what I do."

"I agree. Didn't know Henry was a philosophy maniac."

"He ain't."

"Oh."

"He's a human being."

Henry poured himself a glass of house wine, friends around
the barrel.

"I love you guys."

"We love you too Henry."

"Here's a toast to Henry the Great."

"Beautiful."

Clink.

"Ay Nance!"

"Wha? Yes? Henry Hi. Wha"

"Where da hell is Giovanni, or your husband?"

"He's talkin' to yer wife upstairs."

"She never stop talkin'. She always got a new business scheme.
Now she want to go into th' music business. I said why the hell you
want to know all them sick bastids in Hollywood? She says no, I
want to do Nancy Sinatra type of music. I said who d' hell gon' pay
t' hear dat?"

"Anyone usin the bathroom?"

"Who's next!?"

"I already ordered!"

"You want a drink—"

Giuseppe squirmed in between big sets of legs, under fruit stand cloths, chasing round his imaginary friend, Casper.

"So ay, she go to Brooklyn, get some tattoos, be a feminist. Feeder health food!"

"Throw a raw steak at her kid!"

"I'll kick y' fat ass."

"Next!"

"Punch her husband in the head!"

"Throw a shoe at his—"

"NEXT!"

"Now who's this kid here?"

"He says he looking for his Nonna."

"He ain't run away from home, is he?"

"He said he went out to get some cookies for Nonna with his Communion money and somehow ended up getting lost. Well, at least you won't starve to death here, kid."

"I ate a lot of food today," Giuseppe smiled.

A man from behind the counter appeared dangling thin cuts of something that made Giuseppe's mouth water although he still felt ready to burst. He clutched his chest and made a strange spindling motion, as if to say, "if I eat anymore, it will not be papa smacking me that I fear, but death itself."

"I don't think he can eat no more, Dave."

"Say I know that kid—where's Nonna?"

"We are trying to figure that out."

"She's been getting spiritual advice from that crazy Father Moritz. This could be even worse than that crazy Rasputin and the Queen. I saw somethin' on that th' oth' night. Crazy stuff; really, it is insane what mad clerics can do! But hey, I know you from Holy Communion; my niece was there too. You a fussy little boy, huh Giuseppe?"

"Yeah."

"Is that Vincent over there? He's another one. He passed on sun-dried tomatoes with his Michelangelo sandwich and the next thing you know he's out in the alleyway secretly eating sardines. He should be in an insane asylum. What, kid, you don't like sardines? How about some sardine ice cream?"

"Vincent lost his mind, eating cigars, stealing cheese, addicted to sardines and Vivaldi. I remember when he used to drink thirty espresso a day."

"Sardines stink," offered Giuseppe.

"If it smell bad, it taste bad. You right, kid."

"Scoot in, hey, let the people pass."

"Someone get me eight poundsa speck!"

Now the boy was stuffed beyond measure and tried hiding himself beneath the overnight tarp of a fruit stand; but he was quickly pointed out by a pair of women about Nonna's age, he surmised, who seemed to agree on something before one, clad in denim smock wrecked with powder and scarlet bandana. All at once he was cowering beneath boxes of lemon, glancing mortified at an abstract pillar of denim before him.

"Where are your parents, little one?"

"I'm not here. I'm a ghost."

"Well—do not ghosts have parents?"

He had not seen this coming and revealed himself.

"One minute you're eating speck and gelato, the next you're hiding under the fruit stand! Where are your parents, honey?"

"Papa is out looking for work on the garbage truck. Mama went with him so that she could wait with him and pray the rosary when he was being interviewed."

"And they just left you here!"

"I am staying with Nonna, for the afternoon, but wanted to buy her a present."

"So Nonna is home, in this neighborhood, and you stepped out to buy her a gift?"

"Yes—but then I lost my five-dollar bill."

"How did you lose it?"

"I was lost by where the market starts and an older girl took me to Tino's, and then I think I lost it when I was trying to make it through the crowd. Now I'm trying to get back to Nonna's house. But the money was Communion money, and now I don't want to go back with no money but also no gift. And of course now I am lost, too."

The woman was talking with her friend up by the gleam of an espresso machine, studiously turning a series of seltzer cans that seemed, it appeared, dented beyond reparability.

"Well we know Nonna, and we can make sure you get there. I also have a little job for you, to make your money back."

"You do?"

"If you help us dry the dishes, we'll get you to Nonna's house with your five dollars."

"Yes ma'am."

They led Giuseppe out from beneath the tarped lemons, back into the light of bustling market.

"Come, little one, behind the wall here."

Giuseppe entered a back room vacant save for a sink and some pyramidal crates of cardboard boxes. Some of the illustrations looked familiar, such as the dwarf and the mushroom; others, cast in a cursive gilt of an unfamiliar tongue, uplifted his eyebrows.

"Now here is Susanna, Giuseppe, who helps us on the weekends. Ms. Greco is a theatre student over at the Lincoln Center and will one day be a famous actress.

Indeed, inhaled Giuseppe, she did quite look like one: even in a plain, stained beige t-shirt, cuffed jeans and water repellant boots, the radiance of her tanned face, seemingly unmarred by makeup, could very well have been one from a billboard.

"Well not quite," said Susanna, squatting down to meet her new friend. "But maybe in a couple of years—sure! The sky is the limit!"

"Enjoy!" piped the second of the ladies, lobbing an un-wrapped sponge to Giuseppe.

"How'd you end up scrubbing dishes with me?"

"I was out looking for Nonna's house and then I almost got lost. If I would have kept going, I would have got there, but then I started having snacks everywhere."

"I wish I was having snacks everywhere," said the young woman. "Instead it's just work and then home to memorize my monologue. Here, give me that." She unwrapped the sponge, stuffing the crumpled wrapper into an old brown shoe, and returned the bright yellow rectangle to the boy. "We're getting a new garbage can, and till then I'm using a shoe."

"Not a lot of things can fit into a shoe."

"That is why I—we—must be nimble!"

Susanna took a series of long steps over to a padded heavy metal chair.

"This is sturdy. You can stand on this work in the sink just fine. We don't even have that much to do."

But Giuseppe was unsure about this; for the mountainous dishes beside the theatre student was unlike any brisker set of plates, cups, silverware, and bowls he'd helped with as of late at home.

"We're doing a play at school written by a student all about someone who wins the lottery. You know what the lottery is?"

"Yes. Nonna plays the lottery."

"Does she, now?"

He nodded, receiving a spoon, drying it pristinely before placing it within the vacant rubber piece.

"There is a puppet show," said Susanna, "and I'm the narrator. Now I don't to memorize the script, as I can read it from out of the audience's sight, but it cannot be prerecorded. In the case something goes awry with the puppeteers we don't want the dialogue playing on and destroying everything. So in fact it's ideally best that I do sort of have the script memorized, so that I might be able to adjust or adapt my tone in conjunction with the ventriloquists. Does this make sense?"

"No," Giuseppe admitted.

"Well then you like movies, right?"

"Some."

"While we're working, I'll tell you a story that's going to be a movie. You can picture it in your head while I tell it, and if my calculations are correct, while be finished with the job when it's done, and you can go back to Nonna."

Giuseppe smiled. He accepted a batch of silverware and took to delicately drying each piece, as his new friend spoke in a way that rendered him hypnotized:

"Lorenzo Aquinas Kolbe Lombardigiocoli was born into a whirlwind of expectations he could not afford and went about passing these expectations by like any good young American would. When his math scores were low, rather than extra study-ing, he'd take a girl out on a date instead; when the present made yet another familiarly, circularly historical turn, he'd create his own little history by drinking on the backstreets of Montclair, New Jersey with his high school friends, the way his mother and father had, with whom he lived.

"Lorenzo was bored. His friends came and went, his girl-friends were unreliable and bored with having nothing to do among streets he'd accidentally, nocturnally memorized, he began to work with his father at the second-generation tailor shop. Oc-casionally he'd take a plane out to California to visit relatives and forget about things, but even there things could not be forgotten. Beneath illumined palm trees, uncles would ask, "How's your mother?" and "Where will you got to school next?" and "You still working at yer dad's tailor shop?" and "How does that place stay open?" Obviously distraught, they'd shove twenty dollars in his pocket, pat him on the back, and wish him the best of luck at the bus terminal that led to the desolate airport.

"Childhood had indefinitely ended, gradually and suddenly followed by high school graduation. His father threw a little party for him in the back yard, and a few old friends stopped by to bob for apples and to play chess and to talk about the future drinking beer. One of his friends, Pippy, constantly egged him on into sav-ing hundreds of dollars, and to make it out to Atlantic City with him, to blow it all, or, to win it big.

"'How many times have you gone down there, Pippy?'

"'Ohm at least six or seven, why? You don't believe me? You'll love it."

"'But what's so great about it?'

"'You ever gamble?'

"'No, of course not.'

"'Well, what've you got to lose? We could earn big winnings, I'm telling you!"

"Lorenzo looked at his watch. There really was nothing to lose. His father overheard Pippy and walked over, ice cubes rattling in his tender glass.

"'You fellows want to gamble?'

"Now the crowd began to move away from the bar, and over toward the scene Lorenzo's father was creating.

"'I'll show you how to gamble. I got a poker table in the basement. You don't like poker? Blackjack, 21. Let's play 21. Luck of the draw, no advantages going in, no schemes, no nothing. Everyone's invited down. I'm going to set the table up in ten minutes. It'll be good for anybody interested in the big time.'

"'But I'm not interested in the big time, I just love Atlantic City,' said Pippy.

"'Well then come on downstairs. Lorenzo's never gambled a thing; have you, Lorenzo? You ever gamble before, play some cards, roll some dice?'

"'No, dad.'

"'Well it's time to learn, then.'

An old man chewing an unlit cigar stepped in, apparently a relative of the shopkeeper, whose pregnant center was minimally covered by stray bits of newspaper, chaotic and bent as the man's limited white blades of hair.

"Let them kids take a break from th' dishes; put on d' Yankees game!"

"Break time," smiled Giuseppe's friend.

He took her hand and walked through a curtain, to watch a couple of innings of the game.

V.

AT THE SAME TIME, on the other side of Rodham Road and through the gates, the ability to gather at Professor Vinegar's house right on the corner or Arthur and Bathgate, as opposed to BTNH Hall,[1] engendered the discreet, albeit prestigious group of academic philosophers, with the prospect of a freer speech. This speech would naturally have to align with Prof. Vinegar's views, made clear on the various posters of men, hammers, and sickles framed throughout his mansion, coupled with the extremely high probability of microphones in each room. So in essence nothing interesting would actually happen unless a Socrates of sorts somehow made his way into the famed mansion, which as it went, on this night did happen.

The Philosopher's Reading Group of Rodham University had decided on Milk Vinegar's home due to an incident on campus, when one Terence arrived in a ramshackle state of pills and booze one random Tuesday afternoon, declaring that all academic philosophers were, and I quote, "wolves, hyenas, swine, fools, and madmen."

Now this would not have mattered much as the man had already destroyed his reputation by moving from an orthodox aesthetic Kantianism to a full-fledged support for what amounted to an arsenal of Nazi thinkers: Heidegger, Carl Schmitt, Wagner, and philosophical reflections on Knut Hamsun, Ezra Pound, and Louis Ferdinand Celine did not, at once, draw the ire of the department. None had made the connection. But then it turned out that

1. Bone Thugs 'n Harmony, formerly Martyrs' Hall, of Rodham University.

photographs had surfaced online of Terence with a toothbrush mustache, to which he had, rather than responded with gushing apologies bordering on suicidal thoughts, or worse, public castration, Terence then declared that nothing like six million Jews were killed in World War II. Worse still, he cited academic studies in proving his point, one of them a Jew from the Ivy League. Worst of all, Terence's mother was a Jew, making Terence, at least in accordance with Israeli or Talmudic law, a Jew.

This event particularly infuriated one Noe Bohm, a fourth-year doctoral student, and worse yet, a Jew for Jesus. In Terence's toothbrush mustache Bohm found the perfect symbol of two evils: anti-Jewry meeting anti-Christ, amplified by what amounted to, he believed, self-hatred.

Noe and Terence were screaming at each other in BTNH when Prof. Vinegar at last proposed that this fight be taken elsewhere, preferably his home, where he ultimately intended to have the insane man, Terence, arrested, and a discussion on philosophy's role in confronting hate speech be the topic of the night.

But Terence did not show up, thus vindicating they who lay in waiting for him.

"I knew it," said Noe, blowing his nose, "I knew he was a bigot coward."

"It does not make sense," Linda said. "Why do people turn out this way? The same thing happened to a family friend of mine, Yukio Mishima. Everyone loved him, and then—"

"Oh wait just a minute, Linda," shuffled Noe, "No—please—love is so strong a word. Love? Really?"

"Noe, did we not tell you last time that you need to stop cutting off women? It is really gross. I'm serious, yes, it is gross and very unchristian of you. I understand that you have a brother who is not all that different from Terence Hitler, but that does not—"

The doorbell rang; Prof. Vinegar double-raised his eyebrows, set down his vapor pipe, and left the small group in silence.

"Look, Linda, we'll talk another time about all this. Please forgive me. I pray to the Lord that you forgive me."

"And what if I don't forgive you? Does that mean that this Lord that you speak of has just like decided to not answer that particular prayer?"

"I'm not going to answer such an offensive question."

Then Omar stood, outstretching his hand as though to silence all as Milk reapproached, his face something like a blank slate that seemingly magnified the dirty-looking faint sort of mustache was sort of growing.

"That was UPS. I think Terence sent us a package. But it's from overseas. Rome. What the hell is he doing in Rome?"

"Damn," belched Noe, "What if it's like a bomb?"

"The Lord would not allow such a thing," said Linda, finishing her martini. "Would he?"

"If I knew what the Lord wanted I would be as powerful as the Lord. And since that is not the case, I do not know what to tell you. But I think we should open it. Also, I have to use the restroom."

"That's convenient," said Moshe. Everyone turned to the quiet scholar. "So if the bomb goes off, you'll be down the hall. You have no faith in the one who is beyond language; no wonder you worship a crucified man!"

"My goodness!" cried Professor Vinegar, stepping between them. "Comrades—I thought we were here to escape insanity and violence! Not simply relocate it from BTNH Hall to my house!"

He stood between them with his arms firmly outstretched.

Then suddenly the turned open, and in stepped Tiny Moaf: Tiny had the distinction of being the first-ever master's student of philosophy at Rodham who was also a dwarf. She stepped ahead with an armful of cupcakes in a plastic box; her jubilant presence threw the attendees' cumulative departmental strife into relief.

"Tiny, thank heavens you're here. Oh! And vegan cupcakes!"

"I love vegan cupcakes," said Tiny, handing them to Prof. Vinegar, and patting down her plaid dress.

"I love your dress, Tiny," gushed one of the women.

"Now if anyone wants to smoke, please just do it by the window, if you can."

"Thanks, Milk."

Tiny could hear in the silence of fetched ice-cubes that something was wrong, that she had walked in on a tense situation. And yet she herself may have warranted this very feeling, she reflected, in her recent article denouncing feminism in harsh terms. One line from the article, that it seemed everyone in the room was no recalling, had wagered that if Eve, for all her faults, was merely a rib, then today's western feminists must be something less than a fingernail clipping. Further, she had in her purse not marijuana, but bits and pieces of a science-fiction novel she had made headway into drafting, a good forty pages, entitled *The Mammoth Chamber*.

Over in Paris she had seen a most charming sketch: Rabelais, as a sort of giant, dissecting all of society in his books. She could not—or really needed not—explain how this had propelled her vision, but she had in that moment realized she wanted to dissect the Rodham Philosophy Department: there was something terribly wrong with all of them, and only a type of fiction could indeed render anything remotely close to the truth, or heart, of the matter.

"I saw you at the café earlier," said Milk, handing Tiny a Brooklyn Lager. "Are you working on your master's thesis?"

"There is a lot going on," smiled Tiny, clinking her bottle to Noe's.

"One never sees one writing with pencil these days," said the latter.

"Yes," said Tiny, "That is true."

VI.

MEANWHILE GIUSEPPE WAS EARNING his way out as a free man, enraptured with the actress's play. The further into it he went, the more distant grew the reality that he was in fact breaking the rules in staying out so long, and that the trouble could very well be severe. However, a whooping seemed less serious than the strain he might cause Nonna and his own mama; and thus to move far from this reality and into the narrative theatrics was a joy to the second power.

"A few girls left, a few guys showed up, and another few guys showed up. Lorenzo's stepmother showed up. Everybody had the hots for her. She went straight up to bed, the grouch.

"The sun set. Lorenzo drank a few beers with his friends outside, against the shed. "When do you guys leave for college?' he asked.

"'August late something.'

"'Same.'

"'The 30th.'

"'The 29th.'

"'Same.'

"'You got to come out and hang out, Lorenzo. We'll meet all types of women, and throw parties, and do whatever you want to do.'

"'You can't work at the tailor shop forever," smote Lorenzo.

"'I'm going to check on the gamblers.'

"'We'll be here.'

"A car alarm went off in the distance.

"The basement was filled with smoke and silence, dust filling the air, boxes and boxes of junk creating walls around the table. Four of them sat there, concentratedly.

"'I've won ninety dollars,' said Pippy.

"'Already?'

"'Yeah, why don't you sit down?'

"'The rest of the guys are outside. They'll leave without saying goodbye if I don't check on them periodically. But, you won ten dollars? Why don't you come upstairs?'

"'I can't.'

"'Why not?'

"'I'm winning.'

"Mr. Lombardigiocoli groaned. The other two folded. Lorenzo walked back outside. Now everybody was getting pretty drunk, banging on the shed and singing, spilling the summer all over themselves, laughing, turning the stereo up.

"'This is the best, Lorenzo.'

"'Yeah.'

"'Turn that down a little, the neighbors are terrible.'

"'Forget the neighbors!'

"Unanimous cheers, clinking bottles. Lorenzo grabbed a few chairs and threw hamburgers on the grill. They all burned horribly and Lorenzo ate most of them. The guys sat around, exaggerating. A half hour passed this way, quickly, the music blaring. Lorenzo ran back inside.

"The scenario changed little downstairs, save a strange groan from Pippy.

"'What's the score,' asked Lorenzo.

"'There is no score.'

"'Who's winning?'

"'Nobody.'

"'Me,' Lorenzo's father chimed in. The other two guys nodding helplessly, with drinks wavering close to overflow with each conscious jolt of their hands, and cups therein.

"'How much more have you won, Pippy?'

"'Silence.

"'I'm ten dollars in the hole.'

"'Why don't you come outside, then?'

"'Because I'm losing.'

"Lorenzo's dad set down a spliced hand, smirking. Pippy threw some money on the table. Lorenzo felt embarrassed, and knew that his father was going to keep the money. Lorenzo went upstairs and sat in the kitchen, staring at the calendar, scratching his scalp. A little dandruff fell. The world was so incredible though there never seemed to be anything incredible going on in Lorenzo's life. No sense in gambling. Work tomorrow, full time, with a hangover. Lorenzo threw his empty bottle into the overflowing recycling bin and grabbed an album he'd play for the guys, some old favorites.

"He went outside and the table was broken. The stove's embers were dimming and the shed looked exhausted. They'd all gone elsewhere.

"Lorenzo decided not to become a gambler in the casino or dice rolling sense. Instead he began playing the scratch off lottery. His stepmother began to find piles of tickets in the trash on garbage days.

"'LORENZO!'

"'What?'

"'What are these?' he asked furiously.

"'Lottery tickets. I play the lottery now.'

"'You need a *real* job!'

"'Sir,' said Lorenzo, 'I have a job."

"'Whatever you are doing, it is not working.'

"'Fine. I'll get another job and hold two part time jobs.'

"'Good. And try saving your damn money once in a while. Your life is becoming a pig sty!'

"Lorenzo went out and got a job at a supermarket, bagging groceries. He imagined the job would be fun, relaxed, anything but strenuous. The other employees there were either much older than him or much younger than him, and if they were his age they had children. All of them took the supermarket very seriously, and the men and women who wore red vests told him lies and agitated him every chance they had.

"Hey Lorenzo, we've got a job for you,' Theresa would say, the assistant manager, aging, adjusting her red vest. 'We want you to play security guard. You'll sit in the back while the delivery men come in out and make sure they don't steal anything.'

"'Sounds good.'

"'Follow me.'

"He followed her to the back and sat beside a plate of plastic vegetables. 'James will probably be in and out of here, tell him to give me a call if anything happens.'

"'Who's James?'

"'Day manager.'

"'Oh, ok.'

"Lorenzo sat around, looked at his watch, he'd have to get to the tailor shop in two hours; one hour left as security guard. He made small talk with the delivery men, who'd been travelling all over the east coast signing forms and transporting food. James came out of his office.

"''Tis Lorenzo, our new security guard.'

"Nods; prods.

"'Hey Lorenzo, come with me, I've got a job for you."

"His breath smelled like the memory of wooden shelves in an uncarpeted basement.

"'You bored, Lorenzo?' walking down the hall.

"'No, I'm all right.'

"'Well, I've got a job for you in case you get bored. Here's a rake.' James held the door open for him and led him out to the municipal waste disposal. The colossal dumpster's stench could be clearly, nauseatingly gathered at even a good ten yards away.

"'Oh my,' Lorenzo said, covering his nose. James laughed the gesture off automatically, saying, "And there's a bunch of stuff down there, by the bin, that needs sweeping, if you get a chance.'

"'I wasn't bored inside, though.'

"'Well, I know, we just thought it would be nice to give you some fresh air,' going back inside. Lorenzo looked over the railing at flattened boxes, corroded wiring, banana peel, flies, a needle, and a makeshift umbrella of candy wrappers.

"James poked his head through the door, whispering, 'And I'll handle these guys; call me if you need me.'

"Lorenzo walked to the opposite side of the dock and pulled his turtleneck snuggly up over his nose, bringing it down every thirty seconds or so to reinsert more of the Cracker Jacks he'd housed within his cargo pocket.

"Two days later the temperature dropped dramatically. The night rattled with vicious, whipping winds, and Lorenzo was scheduled to handle the late-night shopping cart organization.

"An hour into the job he was blinded by wind, and subsequently injured himself. The lad sat down, having ripped half the nail off of his big toe after accidentally running it over with a cart.

"Theresa came out and walked towards him, huffing and puffing:

"'WHAT ARE YOU DOING?'

"'Sitting down, taking a break for a second look at my toe—'

"'YOU SIT DOWN WHEN I TELL YOU THAT YOU CAN SIT DOWN.'

"'Half a dozen distant workers gathered outside near the entrance opposite, with others still huddled up by the nearer window, to witness that treatment they had long learned to avoid.

"'Really, Theresa, look at my toe—'

"'NO.'

"Muttering, the rotund manager power-walked back inside.

"By now another man should've been out there helping him, as the late shift required two men, and the winds were enough, if one went on unmoving, to turn one blue. Lorenzo waited ten minutes for his blood-thinner to kick in, which did not help much, before waddling inside furiously in conscious imitation of Theresa, which made coworkers and pedestrian onlookers ecstatic and giddy with the light of looming conflict.

"'Can I at least have a jacket?'

"'A jacket?'

"'One of those raincoats or something from upstairs in the closet.'"

"His poor skin was a type of dark red in spots that made one wince to look at; if such was the protocol for such a shift, a witness might well conjure that a call should subsequently be made to higher management to take better care of the outdoor workers in harsh weather.

"Theresa counted a handful of receipts and said, without looking up, 'The closet's locked.'

"'Haven't you got a key?'

"'James isn't here.'

"Lorenzo went back outside and finished the job alone, mentally prepared himself for the tailor shop which he would rather soon need to take the bus out to.

"When he got back inside of the supermarket to clock out, two slips were on the table. Theresa handed him a pen, saying, 'Please just sign here . . . and . . . here.'

"Two Employee Referral forms. One for misconduct, the other for failure to finish job.

"'James said that the cleaning job was optional.'

"'You'll have to talk to him about that.'

"'And what's the misconduct for?'

"'For being snippy.'

"'My toe was cut; mightn't one snip when bleeding?'

"'If you get another one of these slips written up, you'll be in big trouble, Lorenzo. You'll have to speak to the boss, Oswald. You don't want that to happen, do you?'

"The next day Lorenzo called in and said some serious had happened concerning a chess piece and an eyeball, and never showed up again.

"He kept other part time jobs at big businesses, the easiest places to get hired, and kept blowing his money on lottery tickets, convinced nothing was going to happen. When he worked around food, the managers screamed at him for overcooking and undercooking. When he worked around people, they told him not to act so mopey, to perk up, to enjoy life, because one day you could work your way up to the managerial position. It only took Lynette seven years, right Lynette? Yes, sir. Would you like cream and sugar with that? After his mother convinced him he was worthless, just after his twenty-third birthday, Lorenzo took a bike ride out into town, gazing at the autumn moon and dreaming of how he might make his life more interesting.

"Lorenzo pulled up to the ATM and drained all the one hundred dollars that was in his account. He spent ten dollars on wine, ten on food, and eighty on lottery tickets, scratch off and Powerball. He finally had a day off from work. There could be no better cause for celebration on Earth.

"He scratched off all of the tickets and won a total of five dollars, which he would have to try to get into his account tomorrow afternoon. He drank the wine and fell dead asleep, his face smeared with the blood of Yellow Tail, wrappers littering his floor, a dim lamp flickering in the corner. It was unclear whether he'd dreamt his father screaming at his mother, but it didn't matter much to him, he'd decided, even in his sleep at war with himself for having spent his money on wine and lottery tickets.

"Nothing was going to happen, he dreamt. Until—

"'WAKE UP, LORENZO, WAKE UP!'

"'What? What time is it?'

"'Phone.'

"'8:00 am, on a weekend; Christ.

"'Phone?'

"'OPEN THE DOOR—hold one second please, thank you—LORENZO?'

"'Hello?'

"'Hello, Lorenzo?' wheezed what must have been an older man, with a voice familiar from work:

"'Yes?'

"'I've got good news and I've got bad news.'

"Lorenzo sat up. His parents, still in the doorway, failed absolutely in their apparent attempt to withhold elements of jubilation. He had not seen his parents look this excited in—well—a very long time. And even there, in that little bedroom, before the empty wine bottle, so often a great symbolic piece of material for any physiological jury and mental executioner, but now merely an incidental prop.

"'I don't think I can work today, I'm sick.'

"'No, you don't have to work today; this is Mack Knife from the gas station.'

"'What did I leave there?'

"'A lottery ticket worth four million dollars.

"Lorenzo rubbed his eyes and felt for a moment flashback intoxication from the night before. He pondered if his parents were not drunk themselves, and that all of this just seemed strange.

"'I don't believe you,' he joked, yawning. 'So what is it though—I like to sleep in on weekends.'

"'Bring identification.'

"'This is a set up. A third job? Have I been fired from the grocer for smashing my toe? Really, I should have just stayed in school. I know this is a set up,' fingering his greasy hair. 'But I'll come anyway. I'll be there in a half hour.'

"'OK, Sir!'

"Lorenzo went to the bathroom and washed his face thoroughly. He knew he was not dreaming because when dreams merged with something a little too close to reality he woke himself up at the climax of any given scene. He would have thrashed himself awake even from the deepest sleep at the sound of another phone clicking off on the other end of his line.

"He ate toast and drank ice water. His mother cartwheeled through the kitchen. It was a terrible thing to witness, albeit softened by the fact that it did not make sense.

"A hangover was settling in, his nerves antsy. He fell asleep on the counter. A car alarm woke him up, and he dressed up and hopped on his bicycle.

"The gas station was packed with camera crews, cops, and neighborhood people all desperately wanting to shake Lorenzo's hand. He ignored all of them and walked toward the man waving him inside.

"'What would you like to say to the camera, Lorenzo?'

"Mr. Knife handed him the gigantic cardboard check and a marker. The crowd was cheering him on. Lorenzo signed the check and looked into the camera, mouthing, 'I don't get it.'

"It took two minutes for Lorenzo to absorb what had happened. In that time he ate four peanut butter cups. His wine hangover had not dissolved but was almost completely absent, like a painting in a room that has not been acknowledged in half a dozen years. The family went home and called a few numbers he'd been given and went with the bank that would do things quickly, hopping into his dad's back up car and driving downtown. Some persons he never met took $366,000 of it, but Lorenzo rushed home in time to beat both parents and cover the house in money. He gave them $300,000 and instructed them to have someone get together a list of five prospective homes in upstate New York, one of which he'd settle into, and build a little casino empire, after travelling the world in a private jet.

"He also floated the idea of something called "The Year of Excess", riddled with nightlives famous and notorious alike, perhaps renting a room on the Bowery and starting up a comic book, or a journal dedicated to new detective fiction. In his dreams he sang future memoirs: "I, Lorenzo, had spent one million dollars and remembered little of the experience. But at the end of the day, I missed the pain that had let to a life rather routinely blinded with fancy liquors and ski resorts. I moved back to Montclair, rather than upstate New York, bought an inauspicious three-bedroom home, and reconsidered starting up a gambling enterprise.

"All the while the routine of work was something he'd have enjoyed, if it had been his way, he'd think in front of the fire place, beside old Pippy.

"'I'm going to apply for jobs tomorrow.'

"'Why?'

"'For fun.'

"What about the bar tonight?"

"'Go without me. Here's a thousand dollars.'

"Pippy knelt before his master, then departed.

"Lorenzo walked out to the old grocery store.

"'Lorenzo?' Theresa asked, tilting her head into bifocaled squint. She looked neither older nor wiser, but rather the same blend of incertitude and stupidity multiplied by the numerical equivalent of decay that she had ever been. 'Aren't you a million-aire now?'

"'I went bankrupt. Lose everything'

"'No!" gasped Theresa.

"'Things are terrible. I'm sorry things ended so abruptly last time, Theresa. Are there any positions available?'

"She began to smile, to recapture the possibility of the aspect of power again, however fractional, readjusting her red vest.

"'We may have a position open. Stop by tomorrow.'

"'Thank you so much,' he said, extending his hand jocosely. "It's been a tricky year."

VII.

"THE UNDERGRADUATES ARE STILL dabbling in Hemingway and Faulkner," noted Prof. Doyle, receiving his decaffeinated coffee outside Prince Café. "Which is both reassuring and pathetic at once. You do get the occasional subject, though, who wants to go deeper, into the history of the age, in particular the literary history. One of them was talking to me about Sherwood Anderson the other day, and how disgusting it seemed to her that both Faulkner and Hemingway could have treated old Sherwood the way they day. Thankfully though I did remind her that while the species is in general cruel and disgusting, old Sherwood's Winesburg, Ohio is worth more, in every sense, than the entire bibliographies of Hemingway and Faulkner combined. I do not say this lightly or sporadically but after many years of advanced study. She seemed quite reassured by that, and in fact rushed off to Walsh to go retrieve a copy. I envied her; it is quite the thing to read that gem of a book for the first time."

"Yes, well, Professor Doyle, in truth I do not know either of them all that well. But I shall take your word for it. But now shall we get to this business at hand?"

Raphael Dick, an alumnus of Rodham and once-applicant in the Society of Jesus, was a potentially dangerous man. But he was only dangerous because he did not fall lockstep into whatever the digital newspapers had to say at any given hour. Further, he had often been seen talking in earnest agreement with the veteran characters of Arthur Avenue, which was an extreme taboo as far as collegiate relations went: one cherished the food, drink, and dessert, and despised political implications of an orthodox—that is, somewhat literal—understanding of Catholicism, as much as one walked past the statue of one Christopher Columbus with seething visions compressed within a mind of rage and fire for all he and his had done. That Raphael Dick was anything but hostile in relations transcending the plate itself had made him a marked man; and thus he realized he was a poet.

"Yes, the short fiction book idea. I want to see how your poetry translates into prose!"

1. Comets

2. They

3. The Slavery of the Master

4. Flour

5. Epistle

6. Contempt

7. [Jackson C. Frank]

8. [Goliath]

9. Memory of the Memory

10. Velvet Box

11. Northern Lights (The Astrology of Shakespeare)

12. Trace

13. Autonomy

14. Sheet Music

15. Shantel (black woman w/ daughter ala Abraham)

16. Spell

17. A Hanging

18. Porcelain Strings

19. Proximity (man vs. umbrella)

20. The Anti-Semite

21. Shonqueesha the Violin

22. Gift Certificate Temple

23. Judgment Night

24. Easter Garments

25. The Woman Who Became a Fish

26. Signs

27. Gang

28. Migrant

29. Fences

30. Octopi

31. Mortgage

32. Passover Missiles

33. The Crowd

34. Latter

35. The Idiot

36. Applications

37. The Man Who Wore a Sticker

38. Lot

39. The Brainless Queen

40. House Perfume

41. Freelance Liars

42. King Captive

43. Cave

44. Clay

45. The Seminarian

46. Cowboys and Indians

47. The Widow

48. Follow

49. List

50. The Call of Being

51. The Magicians

52. Accent

53. Exteriority

54. Book Burning

55. The Prostitute's Father

56. Bedridden Dr. Dobbs

57. Taking Care of Business

58. Digital Prisons

59. Remote-Control Bird

60. Fraction

61. Less

62. Tore the Sky

63. Craze My Limbs

64. Restoration

65. Various Traditions

66. Anal Cannons

67. Surgery

68. Flowers

69. Love

70. Now Wait

71. Crumbs

72. Handle

73. Evil Communications

74. Interlaced Rings

75. Cup of Teeth

76. Lightbulb Factory Girl

77. Prelature
78. Carr
79. The Flood
80. Peoples
81. Foam
82. Burst
83. Resurrection
84. The Curmudgeon
85. The Depressed
86. A Brief History of Modal Logic
87. Symbolic Logic
88. Citadel
89. Theories
90. Agency
91. Diabetic Birds
92. Magnetic
93. Dom's Dissolving Arrow
94. Rate
95. Plant-Woman
96. Demiurge
97. Evaporations
98. Paralysis
99. The Ventriloquist
100. Machinations

"The titles are intriguing. But are they just titles?"
"No; the book is complete."
"So you're kind of like testing me?"

"Yeah. I once read Shakespeare to a creative writing seminar without saying it was Shakespeare and I was told it was terrible purple prose and that I should seriously reconsider what I was doing. Ever since then I must test people."

"May I ask what you read to them?"

"No. I mean, you did ask, but asked by implying. It's like when someone asks if they can ask a question. But they just did. So one should ask, 'Can I ask an additional question?' Anyhow, it was a page of *Much Ado About Nothing* and the seventeenth sonnet. As for the former, some of these in the rooms were Ivy League theatre people, mind you."

VIII.

"He returned the next day.

"'We've got an opening Lorenzo, for a few jobs. You remember, Marlena, don't you, our recruiting officer?'

"'Yes, good afternoon Marlena!'

"'Good afternoon, Lorenzo! I'm very sorry for your loss. I've seen many episodes on TV where people lose millions. It happens much more easily than the average person knows. Just confirm this is your signature and you'll be good to go! No training needed!'

"'Yes; this is my file all right.'

"'Great! I'll call Theresa.'

"Lorenzo looked up at the employees of the month.

"'Pleased to meet you, Lorenzo, I'm James.'

"'How do, James?'

"'OK, Lorenzo, we've got a job for you, one that you didn't come through on last time," said James, handing him a rake. "Clean that stuff up below outside by the dumpster for now, and we'll go from there."

"'Sir,' said Lorenzo, 'Don't you think that's a little ridiculous for minimum wage? I would prefer not to wallow in such filth; this is less a job than it is mercenary feudalism, or a public flogging of the soul.'

"'Lorenzo: you wanted another chance, didn't you, I mean, don't you?' snapped James. 'Now I'm sorry for your loss and all, but I would very much prefer if you did not make light of slavery.'

"'To that end, sir,' said Lorenzo, 'Let me take care of the extraneous debris. I believe we've had a communication breakdown.'

"'Let me know if you need anything. We've got outdoor pagers now, here's the code. Type mine in and speak as through a walkie talkie if anything strange happens.'

"'Yes, sir.'

"A glorious day it was. Magnificent sun above, glittering amongst the fluffy, innocent clouds of cotton candy, one hundred sparrows fluttering from tree to tree, children outside beyond the building complex play hopscotch and riding bicycles, elderly women walking handsome puppy dogs, the smell of a boardwalk in the air, the still trees, the leaves of grass with its overwhelming scent of life, of liveliness . . .

"Lorenzo paced the loading dock and drank from his flask. He was drunk in a half hour, pissing all over the municipal waste disposal, and laughing hysterically walked back inside, propping the rake up against the wall.

"'Finished already?'

"'Yes.'

"'Now that wasn't so hard, was it?'

"'Not at all, sir.'

"'Go see Theresa; she's got a job for you.'

"Lorenzo walked through the fruit section, grabbing an apple. He bit right into it, letting juice run down his chin, tucking in some paper towel for a makeshift bib.

"Theresa saw him coming; her glance morphed into a savage returning upward of the head.

"'LORENZO. DID YOU EVEN PAY FOR THAT?'

"'Yes!'

"'That is illegal! And against store policy!

"'A mortal who was hungry from a hard day's work had himself an apple. So what?'

"'*SO WHAT?*'

"'A man's got to eat.'

"'Come upstairs,' Theresa gnashed.

"'I would prefer not to.'

"'Lorenzo—are you drunk?' She said sympathetically, 'That is another matter altogether. I thought I smelt booze there for a second. Let's go to the conference room. I can't imagine the stress you are under, losing all your money . . .'

"'O lady, what I lack in capital I shall make up in chivalric grace. Wilt thou nibble from mine apple, thou pale saint who hath seem so famished in and out?'

Pockets of bystanders had by now meddled together into one vast sea of perplexity. At a glance, one could see the veteran workers of the store sweating, looking over at the obtuse scene, whereas the high school and college students shushed each other from behind recording devices. Then Lorenzo lit a cigarette.

"'WHAT THE HELL IS THIS?'

"'Dame T,' proffered Lorenzo, 'May I wear thy flaxen scarlet vest, and love thee?'

"The apple hit the disinfected ground, swept up by the gloved janitorial hand of a faceless being. A steady stream of tobacco was cut off by the army veteran working in seafood, who with tattooed hand grabbed poor Lorenzo's shoulder, momentarily paralyzing the latter.

"Having recovered feeling, Lorenzo slipped out of the grasp and saw that behind the once-soldier stood James, the managerial force whose presence exclusively connoted things unwell.

"But rather than quiver, Lorenzo looked once into the hopeful eyes of a woman right about his age, herself transfixed with this rebellion against invincible corporatism. She smiled sweetly, and Lorenzo briskly envisioned himself as a Crusader, retrieving the dame en route to Jerusalem.

"A suited shadow stretched across the crime scene floor. Then Lorenzo orally torpedoed a mouthful of fine apple into the face of the manager, the eruption of the crowd and the apple chunks like a collective unscrewed fire hydrant. And through the screaming, swinging, a dialing, Lorenzo slipped through Theresa's hands and ran out the door yelling straight toward the local bus, onto which he hopped on without hesitation, tossing his half cigarette and a hundred dollars to the homeless wanderer in need.

"That evening Lorenzo applied for a telemarketing job he found in the digital newspaper; an appointment was automatically scheduled for the next day.

"He got the job, selling laundry detergent, and in the meanwhile basked in the glory of rum and recollection. He assumed that at some point he would be arrested or fined for, at the very least, smoking inside; and it felt good to know that such fines or bail money for prison were, in the grand scheme of his winnings, something less than pocket change.

"'We think you'll love it here, Lorenzo , and if you stick around long enough we'll give you a fifteen cent raise, and you'll be out of your financial deficit in no time! All calls are prone to monitoring, so read your script verbatim.'

"After a few obviously monitored calls, and a sale to boot, Lorenzo's hand mechanically, without his permission, dipped down at toward his secret flask.

"'Good morning, Mr. Platypus?'

"'It's Plattus.'

"My name Beethoven. I identify as an orchestral dog, and I am running for senator this year. For just the price of a cup of coffee, I'll fight for you—'

"'You're sick.'

"Next call.

"'Good morning, Ms. Fatally?'

"'It's Fallite. Mrs. Fallite—I am married.'

"'I am terribly sorry to hear that, Mrs. Fallite. Well; my name is Mr. Clean. I'm calling on behalf of hygiene. I would like to learn some things about you, so that we can assess which is the best place for your in the years to come. Included is a complimentary issue of *Highlights* magazine.

"'Mr. what? What do you mean hygiene box?'

"'Shlomi Clean.'

"'Your name is Mr. Clean?'

"'Yes, ma'am. Clean. We are calling around town, as we long to ensure that the profane of this town are given a chance at redemption that, hitherto, money could not buy.'

"'I do not understand.'

"'Nothing makes sense. But it is precisely this of what we must talk.'

"'Talk?'

"'Yes. We're using the telephone. Now, about your soul—'

"'It's 8:00 am.'

"'It is never too early for apocalyptic.'

"Next call.

"'Good morning, Mr. Hockabockatrockadockasockamock-alockafockarockadockawockawoo?'

"Next call.

"'Good evening, Madame Ju?'

"'This is Mr. June. It's 8:06 in the morning. Who is this?'

"'My name's Neal Cassady, and I need your help getting to the White House.'

"'Neal Cassady?'

"'Yes, sir. I'm alive. I'm hiding out in Argentina.'

"'Fuck you, man.'

"Next call.

"'Good morning, Mrs. Warmth.'

"'Yes?"

"'This is Peter the Hermit, and I am here with Barack Obama. We want change.'

"'Change we can believe in!'

"'But in order to do get this done we must first tackle the climate crisis. For just forty nine ninety-nine per week, you can help all of the marginalized victims—'

"'WHAT IS THIS?!'

"'A famous politician has recently come out as a lesbian. We want to celebrate this act of courage in style, but we can't do it without you. For the low cost of nineteen dollars and ninety-nine cents per month, you can make the history books. Our plan is ambitious, but together we can make it real: paint the Hoover Dam a rainbow made out of the names of all our donors—'

"Next call.

"'Good morning, Mr. Butts.'

"'Butts?'

"'Good Morning, Mr. Seymour Butts.'

"'That's not who this is.'

"'I know. But I'm going to call you Seymour Butts. Is your refrigerator running? Has your lip shit, lately?'

"'Yes. Are you the pharmacist from up on Westwood Grove?'

"'I beg your pardon.'

"'This is the pharmacist?'

"'Providentially not, although—'

"Lorenzo's screen blinked off, black, all at once.

"'LORENZO WHAT THE HELL ARE DOING!'

"'Hold on, sir, please, hold on.'

"Lorenzo took a greedy nip of his bejeweled flask.

"'Dear me!'

"'What? Let a man drink; life is long if you know how to live it.'

"'GET THE HELL OUT OF HERE BEFORE I CALL THE POLICE! YOU ARE SICK IN THE HEAD, NO WONDER YOU'RE PENNILESS!'

"Walking home, Lorenzo noticed a 'Now Hiring' sign outside of Burger King.

"'I'd love to work here.'

"'When are you available, and, if you don't mind me asking, were you drinking last night?'

"'I'm currently unemployed. I'm not drunk, that's insulting. I can work any job, any time, any place. You will not find a man more dedicated than I.'

"'Didn't you win the lottery a year ago or something? Did you also work here in high school? You seem familiar.'

"'Yes, and yes; I was so much older then. And as for the money, I gave it all away to charity.'

"'Look, I must say: you smell like alcohol.'

"'I don't know what to tell you. Take me or leave me.'

"'You'll be working in the back preparing food; John will show you the ropes. It is simple and can lead to moving up in our corporation, but you must be in a sound frame of mind.'

"'Perfect.'

"Lorenzo took a box of toys off the incoming deliveryman's hands and followed the manager into the cooking area with it.

"'Hey John, how are the people here?'

"'Most are nice, some are nasty as hell.'

"'What do you do to the nasty ones?'

"'Sneeze in their drinks, fart on their hamburgers, that type of thing. Not I, of course, but it is what I hear at holiday parties.'

"'Oh my!'

"'Why? Don't you treat cashiers well?'

"'Undoubtedly . . . I was curious if the myths were true, as last time I was here I lasted all but thirty minutes and never got to learn.'

"'We are all young once. Want a drink?'

"Lorenzo received something that resembled an espresso cup containing that which do not resemble espresso.

"'It's just water. Make sure you drink water regularly. One must drink a lot of water. For now, here, provide your coworkers with the condiments they need when they yell out the meal's number. You see the higher ones are for breakfast items, like butter and syrup, there; and the more traditional condiments right here.'

"Business was slow. Lorenzo pondered if there was not more to life than taking jobs that one did not need. He pondered what it was to need at all.

"Then there was a scene up front:

"'THIS SERVICE SUCKS, YOU'RE ALL PATHETIC, GIVE ME MY DAMNED ORDER AND DON'T SCREW IT UP AGAIN OR I'LL COME BACK THERE AND SO HELP ME GOD GET YOU ALL FIRED—'

"Lorenzo contended that the man did rather look like either a lawyer or a politician he had seen along half a dozen billboards at some hellish season or another in his earlier life. But now the irate man stood screaming at the poor cashier, sweat pouring from his pulsating forehead, the sheer width of the vein trapped beneath the skin of his forehead rather wormlike, and disquieting.

"'Please, let me help here,' said Lorenzo.

"'I've got it,' said the cashier dismally and, vanishing, took the dampened satchels to an unseen place.

"'Every time I come here something is wrong. Years on end. All new workers, same mistakes. It is enough to make one scream.'

"And then soaring through the air, not unlike a football in slow motion, came an aspect of what was assumedly, thought Lorenzo, the bag's vanished contents. A burger, yes, but one covered, dripping, with an unspeakable substance. The store went silent. Someone went so far as to fiddle with the overhead radio volume.

"And then the substance dripping onto the man's shoes, from the hair-drenched vein aboard his forehead; he began trembling, turning red, and reached for may have been a gun . . .

"No, that was a daydream.

"Lorenzo stepped out to the front desk and gave the man a quizzical look.

"'WHO THE HELL ARE YOU?'

"'I am Zorro, come to quell thy violent ejaculations.'

"Lorenzo, up close, noticed he was one of the men who'd called several times, begging for an autograph and miscellaneous favors at the gas station a year ago. He was one of those men whose weekly religious service seemed a pathological recollection of how heinously he had broken all the holy laws all week, only to exit the money-counter's room once more, and begin his wicked manipulations and vile hypocrisies.

"'Oh, and come on, why not go somewhere else? You see we are mortals here, who make mistakes, and apparently guilty of crimes so terrible it is perplexity why you continue to come here at all anyhow. You are the god of your universe, yes, but you are a baby in mine.'

"The regional manager was briskly squeezing through the doorway as Lorenzo donned a paper crown, taking a sip of his dazzling flask.

"Five reorganized bags of food at the edge of the counter fell over and to the dumbfounded man's feet; he could not comprehend how or why Lorenzo was pontificating at Burger King, that hitherto punching bag of a lunch break.

"'LORENZO? WHAT WAS THAT? THAT MAN'S GONNA CALL THE POLICE! CUSTOMER ALWAYS COME FIRST! THE CUSTOMER *ALWAYS* COMES FIRST! YOU›RE . . . FIRED!'

"Lorenzo gathered round his peers. He cut each of them checks for ten thousand dollars, insisted they simply quit this place and start afresh. That redemption transcends vengeance.

"We are told that Lorenzo does so to this day; so be kind to perceivably lesser beings."

As Susanna finished her story Giuseppe came to, observing the completed dishes before him. Now, in addition to getting back to Nonna's house, he would have to get her a lottery ticket. He did not completely understand the story but longed to know someone, especially someone who could share with him, something of a fortune. It would also, of course, eliminate his poor parents' ills, and make every lunch and dinner great, rather than just at holidays.

"Do you think I'm a good actress?"

"Yes, I think you will be famous."

"How about instead of five dollars, then, I give you my autograph?"

"I need the five dollars for a lottery ticket."

She took out a crisp five-dollar bill from her purse.

"You want me to buy you a lottery ticket? Will you keep it safe? You must give it to Nonna when you get in. Say someone gave it to you at school."

"I don't know anyone at school who would have a lottery ticket," Giuseppe said wisely.

The more sprightly of the octogenarians returned through some plastic, linoleum drapes, cradling a dusty rolling pin.

"He wants a lottery ticket as well as the five dollars."

"I did so the dishes perfect."

The three of them walked over to the sink. Giuseppe got up on the crate to overlook his masterful array of glimmering silverwares.

"I never play," said the lady, "But just last week one of our regulars came in giving tickets to everyone. You gotta sit at home at the certain time, tonight I think actually, and check your numbers.

You think you gonna be home in time, Giuseppe, with an old, to watch the numbers with?"

"Yes, miss. From here I'm going to find Nonna's house once and for all, with God's help, at the church across the street."

The older woman smilingly slipped Giuseppe one of a batch of tickets for the evening's lottery. He now had a third incentive to return home, which he privately noted could technically bode well with the Trinity he was learning about in Religion class every Monday night. Between papa's spanking, Nonna's disappointment as well as his mother's, and now the chance to even miss the night reading of the lottery game that would in effect insult the lady who had given him five whole dollars just to make clean some spoons and butter knives that were rather clean to begin with—and listen to another story in a day full of them! His heart was filled with magical reverie as, just about hypnotized by a great harmonious spirit, the beautiful actress took him by the hand outside, down a street quieter than Arthur, as he thought to himself of the Father, Son, and Holy Spirit, each of them walking with them as well.

IX.

FOR THE FIRST TIME in six hours the traffic died down at the bakery. The women compared this to interstellar space travel. It was like traveling at the speed of light, dispensing olive loaf, white chocolate cake, baguettes, loaves, sticks, brownies, scones, croissants, multi-colored cookies by the quarter pound, half-pound, full pound, two pounds, three pounds, little white and red string snipped and tied, refilling wax papers, another vat of coffee, pointing out the napkins, cream, sugar, plastic utensils, the display moving from anarchical to rearranged ever twenty minutes, some Pennsylvania plebeians seeking the only tea then out of stock, wedding cakes, crumb cakes, confirmation cakes, ice cream cakes, gelato, cinnamon loaves, garlic bread, refilling the basket of sample pieces, refilling the little jar of oil beside it, collecting one coin and another from the ground, pockets-ful of dollar bills, torn apron, a broken nail, dying phones, resur-rected phones, a televised soccer game, an unfamiliar politician with a three-beer buzz looking for pizza bread, a one hundred-year-old man wheeled in all smiles, seeking his daily bag of prosciutto bread, unfazed by the festival, wheeled back outside by his devout care-taker, who turning with her black and white cookie signaled the first break all down, sitting down on upturned crates in order to process all that had just happened and all that was perhaps to come.

"I have heard that a man," said one of the bakery girls, smack-ing the powder off her hands upon maroon apron and applying a silk cloth to her eyeglasses, "Who lives on the fourth floor of my building, knows a woman who has contracted the disease."

"Oh no!" gasped her coworker.

"In the past fourteen months this is the only person I have known to contract the disease outside of a coworker and another person, actually two, who did not contract the silent killer in our city, or even state. This pair thought they had the flu; but as all of life is yin and yang, they were to find out that the flu seems to have been eradicated from our lilting civilization altogether, and now are proud, heroic survivors of the outbreak."

"Well it sound like that woman knows that the man was not so lucky.

"In order to stay safe, all of the tenants and I have signed a Pledge of Safety, which is destined to save lives. Essentially, for the remainder of 2021 we have all promised to wear four masks at all times, including while sleeping and in the bathtub. So just in case it seems weird to you please understand that I am saving lives, and making sacrifices . . ." reapplying her eyeglasses through a sneeze. "I am also creating four dozen plastic cubes within which we can safely eat. Three times per day various volunteers go on McDonald's runs, and bring breakfast, lunch, and dinner to tenants, so long as they are safely cubed. The meals are left outside of the cubes and retrieved only when the deliverer is out of the apartment.

"The most disturbing thing, my neighbor who knew the woman who came down with the potentially lethal virus, is that she experienced no signs whatsoever. There is a long list of symptoms which I'm sure you are already aware with by now. Of everything on that list, she felt and exhibited zero. This is the unprecedented reality that we find ourselves in: that the virus that is destroying the world is so secretive that taking out persons left and right without indicating in even the slightest sense that anything is transpiring."

The girls immediately turned back to kneading dough on the long metal countertop, as nearby sounds indicated Jubilee, the owner's daughter and soon-to-be inheritor of it all, waltzed in talking to herself.

"Sanity is boredom," sniffled Jubilee, swiping dandruff traces from her knee of new black spandex. "Why should one let imaginary numbers steadily build while the self steadily decays? One wants carpe diem with a touch of a reason; such is a true joy, like

a man disillusioned with political systems, or one addicted to utopian thinking who was at last been violated, be it robbed or raped,
maybe both. So I say sanity is boredom, really, and the measures
of reasoning are not quite so cut and dry as deductive and induc-
tive, though the subcategories themselves distend into the realm
of the physiology; such is the case of lesser minds, to which smart
technology caters."

"I don't know," Coretta said. "I think the zodiac influenced
the gospel writers."

"No," interjected Johanna, farting, "I swear to Zeus that if I
have to hear about the zodiac one more time this year I am going
to throw myself into the deep fryer. I'll do it."

A shuffling sound tore their collective attention from the re-
flexively waxen break room table.

"That's the new janitor, Pythias."

"Where did your dad find her?"

"She was at the fish market every morning going from room
to room, he told me, trying to sell slip-resistant bags for fish. But
the fish are all boxed up at the place. I don't know, the story does
not really make sense."

"I won't mention no zodiac," huffed Coretta, "But I'm just
sayin'—if we knew her astrological sign this would all make more
sense. Also, I don't think women should be called janitors."

"Um, why not? If one works as a janitor one should be called
a janitor. Don't tell me you're one of those women who would call
yourself an alumna, or actress, right?"

"Gosh, she looks so depressed."

Then the chatter ceased, and a quiet fell upon the inside of
their bakery. All at once the women recalled the tips that had been
dispersed without end, in both cash and on card . . . and as the tal-
lied numbers rose and rose for each of them, it was like air pumped
into a flat tire of the mind . . . who ever thought working in a bakery could be so exhausting? But then one recalled the work of one's
forefathers, foremothers, without air conditioning, without good
clothing, without money, nothing but God alone . . . which in a
sense was, actually, everything.

X.

THE DEFROCKED PRIEST WAS picking through the dumpster out
back when Jubilee, having locked up, said a prayer of thanksgiv-
ing and mercy, genuflected and locked the heavy backdoor and
its double for the night, alleviated by the possibility of vaporizing
hashish tonight in order to ward off the periodically encroaching
ontic death that was the way her suburbs had a demented charm
about them.

At first, unable to see, she made a mental note to have new
parking lot lights reinstalled, and then froze in her tracks to listen
to what she thought was a racoon in the dumpster. And stepping
toward the dumpster she saw a tied-closed plastic bag inside neighboring bushel . . . calcium tablets . . . medication bought but not
taken . . . and then thememory of pouring rain but no umbrella,
of one who had a seeming phobia of umbrellas . . . nowhere in the
world but New York could any of this make sense; and nowhere
but Arthur Avenue could one explain over espresso and a game of
chess why it is better to not use umbrellas.

$$\sim$$

The old house of retired, senior Jesuits out on Rodham Road was
in agreement that there was a particular lot of hoo-ing and wooing
out on the streets below, and throughout the springtime campus,
that night.

"I know the answer now," said Fr. Topper, SJ, tucking away
his homily on "Why God Particularly Loves Non-Whites,

Homosexuals, Transexuals, and non-Christians Revealed," "It is that everything truly makes sense . . . even the bad things. That is the harder part you know, but I am convinced; that even the most terrible things are good."

The poor volunteer before him did not understand his language. Even if the volunteer had, the sentiment would have struck her as incorrect.

"I was there when Father Maddy Pilfer, SJ, shot himself on the altar on Juneteenth, as an act of protest. It was controversial, but his heart was in it. No one is allowed to talk about the incident but that is the way truth goes; great work takes time to be understood. You know?"

The volunteer said smilingly, "Fodder, here your medicine and water."

As she observed the senile man tremblingly take the orange cylinder to his prune-dark, paper-thin lips like a shot glass in the form of a tube, she listened on to varied feminine noises coming out through the closed-blind window. She had been invited to parties but never went; the noises these vain, rich girls made when drunk reminded her of the Guatemalan wilderness: of tribal calls, strange birds, cawing and hawking through the hallucinatory night, aspects of which dwelt within her crystal clear, despite this being the end of her second semester, and ninth month away from that place that had for seventeen years been the sum of reality.

Three seniors pranced by the window. They cupped their hands around their mouths, staggeringly tilted backwards, and cried out for the hundredth time,

"Woo!

"Woo-woo!

"Woo!"

"Oh my God," said Sam, "Like I don't even believe we're doing this. Guys, bro, I like love you all so much. I don't know what I'm going to do without you."

"Woo!"

"Ha! Ha-ha-ha! Hold on—Sean is texting me!"

"God I hate him. I should never have let them do that last weekend."

"You loved it," slurred Kate, "Don't act like you didn't."

The act was on film, sure, and this was distressing.

But still Emily did not know that the entire video had been sold to the second-most famous porn website in the world.

That in a day or two her reputation as a budding corporate lawyer was to be overtaken by "Amateur College Orgy Ten Guys with Crying Trust-Fund——."

"Should I tell her?" laughed Sam.

"No! What—I don't wait—ha-ha-ha, they gave us each eight hundred bucks, rent for a month. She's not even listening; she's going to piss in the bushes again."

She hiked up her skirt and urinated on the little monument which read "Let peace reign on earth" in six languages.

They stood there, stoned and drunk, laughing at the belltower.

The sun quavered, hovered in the brutal heat, then zeroed in on its vanishing point, and there was an invisible aspect to the crowds and all the jam-packed streets. It was not that there were less people out, or that any shop-keeps were raking down their gratings for the night, but a solemnity overtook the streets, like upswept dust entering oblivion, and trickled through the sidewalks into one's conscience. Visions of punishment crept up in Giuseppe's mind, as he trotted behind some family across the street, now more lost than ever. He felt terrible now that he was no longer distracted, and in earnest had no idea how long he had been away. What agonies Nonna and his mama were facing! How his papa would whip him! And how he knew he deserved it—he couldn't been kidnapped, like it said in newspapers! But then he was about knocked off his feet, and the church bells rang out louder than he had ever heard before: he was standing just beneath their tower, adjacent to the rectory. And he knew from religion class that the rectory was a place people went to do church things when it was Saturday evening or Sunday morning.

"I think the Trinity is with us," Giuseppe said to his actress friend.

"You do? You walk slow—want a piggyback ride?"

"OK!"

The radiant girl lugged Giuseppe down Hughes, out to 187th, and turned right, bringing him down as the crosswalk sign turned from red to white.

"I think that your mama must be very proud of you. You are a hard-working boy!"

"Mama does love me and, just so you know, she did say that only I can be her love, her great joy and love; I'm afraid that I can't have girlfriends yet."

"Well," the actress laughed hysterically, "Don't rush it. Come by any weekend if you want to help again. I am always looking to try out my narrating and acting skills on smart ones like you!"

Giuseppe turned, blushing, and bolted up the steps; he darted in through the little space of doorway open as it was just then closing behind the sexton.

The Rodham gal turned around, and bumped right into Fr. Moritz, SJ.

There was a peculiar rumor about the present priest of Our Lady of Mt. Carmel, a jovial man named Father Moritz. It was said that Fr. Moritz had been a Jesuit, and either expelled from the order or disavowed them himself, remaining something of a substitute priest up and down the east coast, covering in parishes during transition periods, of which there had just been one there in the Bronx. The main problem with the rumor, though, was that no one quite knew what the rumor was, except that it had something to do with the gloves Fr. Moritz wore presumably in all seasons, as he had never been seen without them, either through online searches or in person. Townsfolk went out of their way to bump into the new priest when he least expected visitors; even Giuseppe's Nonna had hid out in a particular batch of shaded bushel adjacent to the rectory in order to catch Fr. Moritz return home from Mike's Deli, lock the door behind him, and presumably sit down, whereupon Nonna leapt to the door and began knocking maniacally, in the hope that the poor priest would thrust open the door so fast that his gloves would either be still removed, or half off, at which point Nonna was to grab one of them and lyingly exclaim that she heard the glove had been blessed by the pope himself. But all that happened was that Fr. Moritz opened the door with a pair of gloves so elegant, and seemingly diamond-encrusted white leather with thin streaks of pale purple, golden symbols of keys, mitre, and fish, edged in royal blue, that the poor woman had to make up a lie on top of another lie, and spontaneously told the poor priest that she felt Satan was on her trail. And ever since, she felt terrible about her actions, and developed a great love and care for Fr. Moritz, who thus became a regular topic of mention and conversation around the house on Sunday afternoons.

Nonna had even begun to wonder if Fr. Moritz had been struck with stigmata, which had definitively captured Giuseppe's attention in putting an image to the name. He already knew about Francis of Assisi and Padre Pio, two saints who had, prior to the stigmata, been 'nobodies', or at least persons living life without the auspices of future historical weight

"Hi, Fr. Moritz."

"Godspeed, m' lady. Say, was that Nonna's grandson? He just made his Communion. Is Nonna here?"

"It is a crazy story, Father. But he is looking to get to Nonna's house as soon as possible, though he lost his way . . . he was visiting with his parents, they went out to the papa's job interview, and Nonna is, or was, asleep . . . he wanted to get cookies, and had a plan to have the door or window stay open behind him as he went next door—"

"Ah, yes, pardon me—but quickly I must say that is excellent to hear, as I am due to pay Nonna my weekly visit this evening." The corpulent priest paused, soaked in the pre-evening scene of Belmont. "I'll miss this town, you know. It was always a joy to meet you students, the elders, everyone, really, and I mean everyone . . . but the men of God have become the men of corporate new media, and it profane beyond words. The Lord has something else planned for me . . . but for now real solace can only come through excommunication. So if I don't see you, as I tell everyone, look me up over the years in time; we'll meet again somehow. You have great things before you; God bless you and your family," he said conclusively, proffering benediction.

The Rodham actress gave Father Moritz a hug goodbye, thanking him; he had unquestionably been the favorite of her class. And in a strange way he reminded her Robin Williams in that film *Dead Poets Society*; here as there the protagonist's real crime seemed like it was, in the last analysis, that his heart was greater than his peers, rejecting mechanical motions and luke-warm seasons in pursuit of loving carpe diem of the soul, telling the truth even at the cost of one's career; he was, she thought turning away, a priest among degenerate sycophants.

While this was happening, Giuseppe walked through the enormous, humbling church, taken with the sense of one by holy abracadabra, *poof*, transported into another world. In this world anxieties and terrors dissolved and one did now just focus on holy things, but was in the midst of them; one looked at random up-ward, and to a beautiful tiled Station, the one of Christ carrying the cross: one did not want to avoid suffering at all costs, which was too often a blend of the utopian and the pharmaceutical, but rather prayer ceaselessly for the courage to vigilantly endure hard-ship in their inevitable recurrence.

Or at least, in a boy's way, Giuseppe leant all at once in this vigilant direction, his fears for a moment absolved by the simple being of this most holy place that his forefathers had, with their impoverished holy hands, help build.

As he stood absorbing its scent a distant brisk noise here and there; everything he delicately touched, observed, inhaled, heard, amplified by a holy silence.

He stood on tippy-toe and dipped two fingers into holy wa-ter. Even the unpainted white porcelain of the font was something beyond smooth; everything within the church took on an intoxi-cating life of its own, a beatific sense of wonder and hope that, thought Giuseppe, he could even taste.

He breathed as quietly as possible, seeing far ahead and to the right a pair of nuns praying the rosary. The illuminating heights of the ceiling made him dizzy, weightless; but he feared sitting down and either dropping to the kneeling-cushion too haphazardly, as he had done once before when every turned his way aghast, and secondly to get comfortable and maybe even fall asleep.

Yes, now the day's journey was taking on a quiet, physical dimension; never before had he walked so much, so quickly, for at least some part on his own! He was in a sacred point of a beautiful maze—let it not end by the dear nuns thinking him an orphan!

Just as the sisters prayed on and Giuseppe pondered what he might do next, cognizant that it would soon be getting dark, he felt a little tapping at his foot.

"Hi there," said the church-mouse.

Dumbfounded, and if we are honest for a moment aghast, Giuseppe believed neither what he saw nor heard.

He squinted down and double-checked that he was seeing correctly. And it did in fact appear a mouse, which was in a sense somewhat cute now that one was not chasing it with a broom or something more malevolent, had not only tapped him on the foot to get his attention, but had spoken to him.

"Are you . . . a mouse?" whispered Giuseppe.

"I am Lawrence, the church-mouse," said the little creature. "Didn't Fr. Moritz tell you that Luigi Giusanni once called the animals mankind's little brothers and sisters?"

"I don't know Fr. Moritz, but Nonna does," whispered the boy.

He stared downward, transfixed.

"I see," the mouse said pleasantly, taking what appeared a brisk note into a microscopic notepad, with an equally microscopic pencil. "I take care of the minuscule things our sexton can't see, nooks and crannies, in exchange for room, board, and cheese rations. Speaking of cheese, would you mind checking your pockets for any crumbs? I can smell good cheese; Casa Della?"

"One second . . ."

Sure enough, Giuseppe found crumbs of cheese and others pinches of miscellaneous edible items throughout his various pockets.

In a strange way, as the church-mouse looked up at him with a smile, the boy grew accustomed to the talking mouse. He felt a wave of comfort overtake him, not unlike that of his father's confirmative eyes earlier, or even some of the pages of the actress's script, which seemed to tranquilize, settle his soul . . .

But could the same be said for a talking church-mouse?

"Do you live here with your family, Lawrence?" he asked, bending down with his crumbs.

"Lo! Here, kind friend, please sprinkle thy tidings along this, my makeshift cart."

The church-mouse set down before him a hitherto invisible sliver of scotch tape, about the size of a fingernail trimming. "I'll explain my living situation in a moment. First, I'll collect the offerings there, then carry back the foodstuff to my, our living quarters."

Giuseppe calculatedly helping Lawrence get the tiny bits of food onto the sliver of tape, leaving enough room for the mouse to, he assumed, in time stick his little hand to the free decimeter of sticky-side tape, in order to drag his potluck potpourri . . . somewhere . . .

"Good. What a feast that is! A wreathed banquet! But yes, I, Brother Lawrence, am a celibate friar minor. I tend to the church's less visible needs along with some others: birds, kittens, squirrels, and even a baby turtle once. We strive for a life free from sin, where every day builds upon the former into a great big harmony of order."

"Aren't you afraid someone might squish you, or hire someone to take you out?"

"Of course not!"

"But how can you be so confident? You're just a little mouse!"

"Well, consider a highway. Do you know what a highway is, Giuseppe?"

"Of cour—hey, wait! How did you know my name?!"

"I know Nonna."

"What were you saying about a highway?"

"Well you wouldn't try to cross one on foot, would you?"

"No!"

"Same for me. I come out when all traffic is over."

"But what do you do . . . If people burst in unexpectedly?"

The mouse pointed to a corner table, with bulletins, donated eyeglasses, prayer cards, and a lost and found.

"See the umbrella holder underneath?"

Sure enough, though invisible to the naked eye, was such a contraption.

"Now look behind."

There was a tiny sign, much to Giuseppe's delight, about the size of a matchbook:

BROTHER LAWRENCE AND THE LITTLE FRIENDS OF CARMEL—TREAT EVERY GUEST LIKE CHRIST HIMSELF—THIS SUNDAY A READING OF ST JOHN OF THE CROSS AT MEATBALL POTLUCK—MUSIC BY ISABELLA THE BIRD AND THE BELMONTS—PEPPERONI RAFFLE

"If you know of any potential donors we are trying to redo the entrance there . . . It is a little banged up. But even that in this city is so expensive! We have been collecting money all year and still only have fifteen pennies! We need a trustful calligrapher!"

"As soon as I have some money, Lawrence, I'll help."

"God bless you! You have a heart of gold. There are great things in store for you, Giuseppe. You and your family."

"Really?"

The church-mouse scurried up to Giuseppe's sneaker and hugged his dangling shoelace.

Before he could even watch the church-mouse delicately burst with his strip of food behind the umbrella basket and into the miniature friary, the main heavy doors of the church swung open, bringing into Giuseppe's perimeter a gust of summer breeze that rendered Giuseppe acutely aware that he must continue on his way.

He bowed, slid into a pew, knelt without cushion. Then he genuflected, little hands folded before the hymnal holder, the very top of his head barely leaning against the smooth oaken curvature of the pew before him.

XI.

BUT ACROSS THE STREET there must have been an afternoon party in some room or another, as the building's entranceway was a maze of debris. In order to get anywhere near the doorbells, one squirmed through a maze of garbage in moving from the eroded gate in through the main door, and once inside lunged over a minefield of broken glass, children's toys, footwear unfit for even donation, and rows of minor celebrities and their autographs within framed squares. All one had to do, however, in order to get to Willard's place, was get through the first sequence of near-garbage and into the third down on the left.

For it was here that the morbidly obese Willard Cowley held court, while the feast paraded on outside in the light of joy, Cowley paralyzed from the waist down, receiving new and regular gamblers into his anonymous abode. But their gambling was not any regular sort: what they gambled on was Willard's ability to hear any given song, pulled up online, and his ability to guess—know?—whether the composer or artist was alive or dead.

The simplicity of it all was deceiving. For instance, an artist killed yesterday with a song that utilized clearly modern techniques had nothing about it that sounded dated. On the other hand, where classical music was concerned, one did not simply summon Beethoven and prompt Willard to obviously suggest the composer was dead: rather, someone could earlier in the week bring over a 1935 remastered recording of Wagner by a composer dead nearly as long as Wagner himself, and then later in the week offer a recording that, unless one was a professional musician or critic, would be rather positive the recording was exactly the same.

This was all made stranger by the fact that it was clear that Eliot Macintyre had no cultural hobbies or interests. Frankly, he despised all culture; it could be said he despised the idea of contemporary culture and worked from there. But he did not despise its very foundations because he felt that some other age was actually a better culture. Like persons, Eliot seemed to despise all equally; his hatred for various genres and skin colors were fixed in their foundations, as cultures, or as beings.

When his mother died, he lost all contact with the outside world. Granted, he had not maintained much contact with it beforehand. He was one of the rare Rodham University students up in the Bronx that was actually from the neighborhood. Better—or worse, depending on whom one asked—yet, he did not leave his mother's apartment upon completion of his undergraduate degree.

There were theories about Eliot, though Mr. Mly, walking down Arthur Avenue to his apartment, theories about his rants that were not really rants, but rather thoughtful, occasional meditations. Mr. Mly believed they were called rants because it was psychically impossible for any of his visitors except Mr. Mly to comprehend such eloquent decimations of all idols. He was much more helpful than any of the philosophers Mr. Mly had ever met in my admittedly sprite albeit legitimate time as a professor of the history of philosophy.

When Mr. Mly was living across the alleyway from Eliot back when he was first paralyzed, he often shared his remaining pastries with him. Things were going unwell around the time Prof. Mly signed off on the Harlem apartment without his being there. Mr. Mly had not wanted to live in Harlem. And in the process of trying to find a place where he could work on his medieval cookbook in peace, Mr. Mly found his rooms in the Bronx, a stone's throw from Nonna's place.

"He was very fond of rainbow cookies and told me once that a specific bakery makes St. Joseph pastries year-round for specific customers, although I cannot say more about the matter lest I get

into trouble," thought Mr. Mly, recalling better days while squeezing sideways through the trammeled fortress of trash and flies.
"Eliot found that the type of society that procures a man who is
willing to compromise insofar as he would proceed (that is, pathologically and incrementally), would do so beside a legion of victims whose elevation was not due to natural gifts but a historical
poverty of them. Anyone proclaiming otherwise, Eliot wagered,
had simply not spent any time in their genealogical homelands.
Therefore, he said, changing holiday names, laws, making society
unrecognizable . . . was not progression at all, but actually archaic
pagan sacrifice. The ventriloquists convince their willing apes of
wrath that a sacrifice of the living will cure their interior ills; but
such is permanent misery, hatred of reality, hatred of one's people
and oneself, the pathology of contagious barbarism and its coun-
terpart, mental retardation.

"Meanwhile, then as now, I was just getting started in my
orphic liturgies. I had come to the conclusion, between consulting
my ultra-orthodox rabbi and eating too many cookies with Eliot,
that women's faces actually look quite like men's, when you look
at the face alone. When you concentrate on them, that is. One can
even get some photographs together, create a sort of rectangle with
one's index, pointer fingers and thumb, and render visible the face
alone. One can never look at long hair and makeup the same again.
Stripped of automatic dividends, or ornamental obfuscations, fe-
males rather look like males. Thus in my shattered mind did I reconsider the wig that had arrived by post from Jerusalem; I wrote
an orphic hymn that evening, three nights prior, entitled "The Cult
of Jerusalem" that was supposed to be a part of my cookbook . . .

"I was on my way to the metempsychosist's apartment, yes,
when I recalled his most recent plight: that some of his visitors
were now beginning to grow suspicious of his magical talent, that
of perfectly knowing that life/death status of any given voice by
recording, sans prior knowledge: it was something of a formalistic
hypnotism, a magic flute for the eyes.

"The group of them (all men from the city but none from
the Bronx; all women from Bronx and beyond in the city were

appalled at the suggestion that the morbidly obese paralytic was practicing black magick) emailed me their conclusions: "Notice, Professor Dionysius, that his window is open in all seasons—yes, he has an electronic fireplace, but it still does not make sense on a February night in a blizzard; combine this with the fact that maybe his neighbor, the guy who moved in after you, has an audio reading app—I know you hate technology[1] but it means that when a song is playing someone can put their phone next to it and the phone tells them what it is; Eliot could then have the person with the phone step out to their car and do the horn (of varying length) once for living twice for dead, or something like that; likewise, this person looking up the song with their phone could then also have the option of yelling 'no!' out of neighboring window if the given artist on the recording was dead—this would explain why it always took Eliot anywhere from five to ten minutes of 'meditation' to come up with his diagnosis."

Sick with the scent of, presumably, rotting food and soiled garments, Mr. Mly sat down in the broken old-fashioned elevator, pulling closed the door before him, in order to drink water and get the rancid smell out of his nose. He genuflected.

"Lord, I was almost shocked when I read this email. Almost, because I long ago learned to curb the emotions, or really put them through the furnace of unrestrained skepticism and cosmic pessimism, in order to dry them out sufficiently for water, to become like unto a tree of dreams. So I was *near* shocked, but only because I understand that nothing is impossible; and this was itself the outcome of a mind-breaking decade of rigorous logical investigations.

But the jig was up, because in fact the men had guessed correctly. Eliot had developed the game after it had become impossible for him to perform the basic motor skills necessary for even the most rudimentary of functions, as in a streetsweeper or

---

1. Lord, I hath a footnote to one aspect of my prayer, concerning which I pray ye do not mind: for the record, I later delivered extreme reprimands to these students for their innocuous failure to ever differentiate between hatred and skepticism, technology and digitality; I had to beat each one of them with a stick I named (Sic)-the-Stick. For other occasion I keep close at hand a red-hot poker entitled "The Staff of Golden Straw."

Joseph Nicolello

security guard, and in his own words, "I took philosophy so far that it became impossible for me to care about philosophy. Then it was a snowball effect, and I lost all interest in artworks too. I longed to do nothing but sit still in solitude and think about how depressing it was, is to be alive; and the gods willed it."

⌒

"The old lady next door won the lottery," said Eliot.

"I heard. Nonna; maybe she'll give you a cut?"

"No. Money changes everything. One with money cannot remember what it is like to not have money and what one would have done with money had one a bit of it, back when it was unfathomable. But now I have one final favor to ask, my lord."

"Yes?" I asked.

"I need you to fill a bowl with water."

Mr. Mly stood. He asked Eliot why, absentmindedly scratching his armpit.

"Because the delivery woman . . . I ate her."

Mr. Mly turned around and looked over his friend's corpulent frame, forearms the size of one's thighs, stretched clothing stained with condiments and sweat.

He swallowed nervously.

Within the kitchenette, Mly found a fish bowl ready. He did not wonder long how it had gotten there. What he wondered was if the students who had written him that letter were in fact anywhere nearby. He looked at the clock, but it was broken. For a moment it seemed as though all of his life leading into this second had been an autopilot endeavor, that even what had seemed like forays into consciousness and the limits of thought were nothing more than sallow cutouts of actual things, concepts proclaiming to be more than concepts: one cannot theorize one's self into a place of existential readiness. No. That takes either death itself, or initiation.

But then a flash of light—underwhelming though at the same time fragrant—flashed across the unused shelves. The fishbowl was filled with filtered water; who had applied that filter to the sink?

Mly picked up the fish and put it into the bowl. He took a microscope and noticed miniature fragments of Eliot's clothing falling to the floor of the bowl, nothing more than dust specks to the naked eye.

"Immanuel," gurgled a voice.

"Eliot? Is that you speaking?"

"Yes," the man-fish gurgled, "And thank you for not being too caught off guard. I'm trying to put myself in your shoes and this now seems seriously fucked up, me turning into a fish and all. Come up with something good for the guys who caught onto us. There's about eighty grand in cash in the oven, in a briefcase. Take it, do whatever you want with it. Only one catch."

"What is it?" Mr. Mly asked the fish, now darting about the polished kitchen quarters.

"I need you to take me to the ocean. Didn't Augustine say that the world is a book and if you don't travel you only see like one page, or chapter, of the book?"

"He did," Mly acquiesced, "Although I am unsure this would apply to a man who has turned into a fish, making the request of an orphic priest."

And yet without hesitation Mly decided on the biggest Ziploc bag he could find down at the dollar store on Arthur, to cradle the bag of water well, and take a cab out to the Atlantic, and set Eliot free at last.

He recalled in prayer:

"As I stepped out, Lord, into the maze of garbage, I ran right into Nonna. I was surprised at how merry she seemed, as I could only imagine how many persons had implied as of late that maybe she could give them some money, now that she had so much of it, and would be moving somewhere exotic soon.

"Nonna, hath thou a sandwich bag?"

"Oh!" she piped, "Giuseppe, go get me a bag!"

The little boy—I take it her grandson—appeared with a clear bag almost the size of an upturned mailbox.

"No, no, not da big one—"

"Actually yes! I am packing a big sandwich!"

I bade her and the boy a genuflection, turning back into El-iot's abode to prepare my, our escape.

"The money," said the scaled metempsychosist.

"I decided on Jones Beach. It seemed like it would take long enough for me to ponder to myself all the way down if I was in-deed witness to reincarnation. At the same time, I tried to men-tally communicate with the fish, but I believe he was sleeping. I kept a half-filled bottle of water in my attaché, in the case that a sharp turn or extreme pothole should result in a movement that ultimately tore open the Ziploc bag. Meanwhile, the driver never once asked just why I had the fish with me, although I suppose it was none of his business, and he had seen much stranger things. "The beach was empty at sundown due to the blast of cold wind that day. Still, it was strange that no one else had thought to even walk along the shore. Nonetheless, Eliot demanded I release him, and so I did.

"To my horror he was at once eaten up by a shark. And thus it was a matter, now, of what became of the shark, if it was a shark at all."

～

As Mr. Mly continued his prayers in the antique elevator, a pair of graduate students prepared to disrupt the collegiate festivities stopped in the apartment hall to discuss matters concerning life and death, life and faith, war and peace, war and war:

"In a brief essay Bertrand Russell once appealed to the emo-tive mob and went against men who are against women . . . but now—wait, let me finish like—I would like to counter this frivo-lous appeal in reconsidering men without women. We shall see that they are, in an age that would glorify the spinster, well within the bounds of sense."

"I remain convinced that yours are the sorrows of Priapus and their sole extinguishing: such is one epiphanic instance of reason that is incontrovertible. By the way of that which no woman can comprehend, ejaculation, man lives his days in a state of seemingly immovable animal desire that is all too often, instantaneously, proven the phantom of a shadow of grandeur. There are thus five models I will now gloss who did not have wives, and did not, it seems, think much of women."

"Well Kant of course . . . Kant gives us a perfect instance of pure mind, twice over, in his life and in his life. You must read the green biography—a call to cultivate one's own mind. For one does not become a philosopher by enrolling in a philosophy course; but one who is willing to submit to a mentor for the sake of casting down ignorance has thereby engaged in a philosophical movement that is more than the masses can claim. Furthermore, whether one is a certified philosopher is in the philosophical (and not academical) sense itself irrelevant. My paper is concerned less with making a living than man's place in the cosmos, and what he might do in the aftermath of a most Miltonic Fall . . . that is the Dantean Hell of self, or the self incapable of responsibility . . . it searches out everything on earth and heaven to blame when the type is in a lonely place . . . but never once does it occur to them that perhaps it is they who are the foundation of a life mired by various crises . . ."

"That is why at the conference we must not forget what Dionysius taught us at the tavern about Flaubert, Schopenhauer (as Schopenhauer remarked on the New Testament . . .), John the Baptist (Hitler had Chamberlain, and Christ had John the Baptist), Jesus of Nazareth In an age when so many are gravely mistaken about Christ, conflating him with the contemporary myth of Judaism, as in a distant family member of mine no one reads anymore, Arthur Koestler, and greatest source of comedy that is for reasons unbeknownst to me neglected; of course I am talking about the century-by-century list of Judaic messianic claimants, or men who claim to be the messiah each century. I am surprised no one has written a novel about this in twenty dense chapters . . . my God it is the real divine comedy . . . but then are we not much better, lest we turn in earnest to the Word Incarnate? It is so easy to condemn others that it becomes as burdensome to continue doing it as would be a full-time job one needed and despised in one fell swoop . . . we should aim for the heights, the riches, the treasures of philosophy . . ."

"To aim high . . . imperceptibly high . . . on the way to language . . ."

"God, please help me get to Nonna's house before she wakes up. I know I have been bad. But please, Lord, please let them know my heart is pure! Please look out for all of the new friends I made today! Please help me!"

The boy bolted upright, genuflected, and bolted back out of the pew.

However, he hit something of a cushioned wall.

"Are you OK, m' lad?"

Giuseppe looked up and saw perhaps the fattest priest he had ever seen in his life. No, this was without question the fattest. And yet there was something kind and caring about his round face, which presently emitted a suppressed belch.

"Be ye not afraid. It is I, Fr. Moritz. And you, little one, let me tell you straight out: Nonna awakens at moonrise, and it is nearly moonrise. Now, come on—she is not far away, and we may very well get there before she awakens. Step to it!"

Now this was a sight to behold, the collective witnesses of Fr. Moritz pacing down 187th Street with little Giuseppe agreed right at that moment and for years to come. Fr. Moritz looked quite flush in the face, his shopping bag and attaché practically the size of galloping boy beside him, the little chattering companions asking him rapid-fire questions about life and faith.

"And then when we sometimes sneak a piece of candy, what about that?"

"Obey the commandments my boy, and keep doing what you're doing, and God will provide."

"Today though is not like me, I am a good student and top of my class, and mama is so proud of me! I don't want to see her cry!"

"Obey the commandments my boy, and keep doing what you're doing, and God will provide."

"What's in your bag? Are you Father Moritz? Have you known Nonna for a long time?"

"Quick, boy—we must cross fast to Hughes. I have a pit-stop for one of my subjects in spiritual direction. We have no time to lose."

The robust priest's belly let out a growl so loud Giuseppe heard it over the flurry of dispersing automobiles coming each which way.

"Are you hungry, Fr. Moritz? Nonna always has something nice to eat! I ate like a king today! What are you thinking about? Is it true that papa said once, that he said, I mean, that I ask too many questions? He told me it was good and that he loved me and that with my studies I would make the family proud, but sometimes my questions got crazy and went too far, and is this true? Can you tell me, Father?"

"Obey the commandments my little Socrates, and keep doing what you're doing, and God will provide."

The ecstatic little boy and his big clerical friend hooked right on Hughes, parting a sea of pigeons.

'Another character!' cried Giuseppe within his mind. "I've never seen people like this before!'

Out came what he assumed was some type of artist or professor, as he looked different from the others the boy had seen on his adventure, and reminded him in a strange unexplainable way of the little film they had watched in Art class on the various painters.

"Good evening, sir," said Fr. Moritz. "I cannot stay long, as it seems like both of our schedules have gotten crazy today. Also, I am to return Giuseppe here, Nonna's grandson, home very shortly."

The poet lifted his black hat, something like the rings of Saturn, and bowed to the awestruck little one.

"The library is my home," said the poet, "And my home is in fact my home-away-from-home."

"I can see you do not get out much. A ceramic shade of pale!"

"Such are the angels who follow me everywhere, and watch over me, and for whom I compose my hymns. Some of our efforts are made known in the City of Man; but all that is worth keeping ends up in the City of God."

Giuseppe accepted a stick of chewing gum from the man, absorbing the fixed, fascinated looks of passersby at this crew of characters before them.

A puppy dog twinkled into the remnants of a rectangularly gated garden.

"I will not argue," Fr. Moritz stated. "But now, as you have so wisely followed my counsels and maxims, have you any advice for our friend here? I am told he is quite the budding scholar himself!"

"I thought I saw him with his parents over by Gino's earlier, with some crazy woman yelling out the window about the Son of Man coming through the sky—"

"That was Nonna!"

"Nonna . . . the seer."

"But anyhow, I must get this boy home. Perhaps you can write a poem for the church one day."

"Father, I am very poor. If you could perhaps guide me in the way of a food pantry, or any poverty relief services, I would be obliged to write you, or the church, a poem."

"Here, take my card." Fr. Moritz handed him what appeared a crayoned blue phone number atop a torn piece of charcoal-colored construction paper. "I too am poor, and had to make my own business cards with materials from the children's school. We shall have a food pantry open this weekend; call me for the precise details, as they escape my mind just now. Oh, and I meant to ask—whatever happened to that woman you were seeing? How are things?"

"It is perhaps too difficult to explain, let alone live. She is coming over this evening, and in fact is supposedly around the corner or at least I thought she was. We may just proceed after all as friends in the Lord. Her little girl is about this one's age, Giuseppe's."

Giuseppe blushed.

Then the poet's arm bolted outward and waved to a forthcoming woman with a girl who was, indeed, just about the same size and age as Giuseppe. She wore a Catholic schoolgirl's uniform with her hair in a black velvet band; tugging her forward was a little dog, somewhere between puppy size and grown into what would, essentially, be not much bigger than a puppy even at full size.

Giuseppe played with the little dog, who was quite fond of our friend. The mother held her index finger before her lips to the children, eavesdropping from two steps away on the conversation between the becloaked pair of poet and priest:

"The concept of history is interesting in so far as the aesthetic, particularly literary vision, of man is concerned; this I say, Father, that machinic acceleration lends itself to a decimation of interior cultivation, while there is a perpetual movement to keep populations on the brink of civil war, in a chaotic bondage, so that they cannot unite and overthrow their masters, whom they enormously outnumber."

"Interestingly, though, on the occasion that the masses overthrow their masters, it appears to either be funded by obscure oligarchical sources or, even it has a more organic flavor, nevertheless ends up in a worse state than that which it overthrew in the fanatical conviction of a utopian better way of living to come. Thus, whether or not a population awakens to the ever-present prospect of oligarchical ventriloquism, its condition is malignant. Hence the goodness in aesthetics and literary history; this is the history of going against the current of groupthink, providing its own history of being, in a realm that when executed most superbly ushers in a level of perception that transcends church dogmatics of geographical religion and political in one fell swoop.

"I was given to providing them with all sorts of names," said the poet. "I began with Pseudo Dionysius's mystical names then dabbled in Jewish mysticism. But in the end, I realized it was just a good gang of baby cats and dogs being protected by their friends, parents, humans like yrstruly and then the elder felines and bitches, and thus collectively named them the Last Kantians of Belmont."

"These then are the famous kittens, the last Kantians of Belmont," the priest said visibly overfilled with joy.

There stood the makeshift crew, at the young poet's gate: seven little kittens peeking out from the remnants of some type of downturned aluminum wall, within which was a series of beds it appeared the poet made. And behind them all, like one of the kittens save twice as big, stood the mama cat, peering out with bright citrus-colored eyes; the poet stepped back to her and the mama cat approached, pressing her little head against his cape.

Meanwhile, the girl's puppy dog sat attentively, wagging its tail in a well-trained silence, swooshing against some bags of things from Tino's and Madonia. Giuseppe was ecstatic in the most bewildered sense, and for a moment lost all track of time and space; there was a real magic to Nonna's neighborhood, he knew, even at his foot an antique book, atop which stood little figurines of a cherubim and Padre Pio; and all these mystical stories!

"We took your advice, Father, and read Sertillanges; about fifty-something pages in he glosses the merits of like-minded people coming together, or at least trying to come together, in the name of the good. And thus here we are."

"That is the spirit, guided by the Trinity," Fr. Moritz said conclusively.

"I was right!" peeped Giuseppe.

The new friends bid farewell to one another as Father Moritz guided Giuseppe back the other way down Hughes.

"Now my son, I must ask, but I need your honesty—if you are not honest Nonna will be very angry with me."

"Yes?"

He looked up, caught within the enormous shadow of the priest, in awe.

"I am very much tempted to stop into one of these shops and stock up on pepperoni and cheese before they close. But I am also supposed to be on a diet."

"You are?"

"Well yes, technically. In fact the diet started just this morning. But lo, I was at once so busy with parish affairs that I forgot, and accidentally feasted on ravioli with two loaves of bread and a small bottle of oil. And thus I believe that, at this point, it would be practical to just keep eating, seeing as I have, accidentally, already spoiled the diet."

"I won't tell anyone," piped Giuseppe. "I ate by accident a lot of food today, too."

"Bless you, child; may ye inherit the earth. Now one moment."

Giuseppe was shocked to see they were all at once in front of Tino's. He peered inside at all the beautiful artwork, the busts of what appeared Roman emperors, fine oaken tables, gelato stand, display of cakes, and a surreal number of meats, cheeses, drinks, candies—all from Italy!

Fr. Moritz reemerged through the twinkling door.

"All set, my boy. Now, to Nonna's house!"

As Giuseppe and Fr. Moritz approached Gino's, neared in on Nonna's apartment building, the boy began to wonder how it was possible he could have ever missed it. It did not make sense; but the notion of nonsense then gave way to an understanding of God guiding him, by way of Fr. Moritz, the robust priest with gloved hands in the summer.

"We might say," began Fr. Moritz, stopping some steps from the familiar door, "That you were by the window, waving to a dog, when its owner whisperingly asked that you might watch it, for the the lady had to run into Gino's for cannoli. Having watched the dog, the owner thanked you for your windowside services with first a piece of prosciutto bread, then a piece of white chocolate bread, which is the reason you are full, in addition to a lottery ticket. Then you got the hiccups, and did not want to awaken Nonna, but a classmate had told you that thinking tap water is vulgar. Thus you stepped out for the bodega, hoping that a wedge of market circulars might keep the door ajar. Naturally, the wind had other plans. That is where I come in and having recognized you checked in to see you were OK; then a parishioner was walking out, who let us in, and here we are."

"It's complicated," said the boy. "I don't know what you're saying!"

"I'll take care of it," Fr. Moritz said. "Let's say a little prayer before we go in."

Having prayed, the odd couple looked up; the front door fell open.

"Hello Father!" said the man from the hardware store. "It's damn hot outside."

"Indeed, sir; we are here to check in on Nonna."

"Oh yes, Nonna—give her my love! See you Sunday!"

Giuseppe walked behind the priest, trying to still the storm of details and concept that Fr. Moritz had just gesticulated. It did seem to make sense as he was saying it, though the boy; but then when he had finished the words did something like evaporate.

"I'll take care of those details," whispered Fr. Moritz, his enormous frame waddlingly stalled before the familiar door. "You just go in and say 'Nonna, Fr. Moritz is here to say hello, to check in.'"

"OK," said Giuseppe.

He walked in as Fr. Moritz stood in the doorway, eyeing a box of cookies.

Giuseppe heard something like the sound of a paw dividing the interior aluminum bag, lightly humming "Come all ye faithful" to himself.

As Giuseppe approached Nonna he found all of his oxygen tucked in through his nose, approaching the great lady in her great chair, who did not budge.

Giuseppe, still breathlessly, swallowed; then his arm was extended toward the drawer, within which he longed to replace the money. Indeed, Nonna was snoring; but did the drawer make clanky, groaning noises as Giuseppe seemed to recall? Or was that just Fr. Moritz off in the distance, treating himself to fresh-baked cookies from Morrone with a dash of milk?

The wooden drawer, with its fine wavering designs strewn across it like little clouds, or smokestack fumes, was indeed well-oiled. Like a television set on mute he witnessed the movement of things without absorbing any sound.

Then the funds were reimbursed, and the old, framed picture of the Lord looked down on Giuseppe with what transformed into a knowing grace of approval.

"I did not know that paintings were alive," thought the boy.

He placed an index finger into Nonna's shoulder.

"Dear me!" she said, though still appeared unconscious, if not dreaming. "Now who is the beggarly sneak? Who was it?"

Giuseppe gulped.

But it was a dream, he observed, as Nonna came to life with a simultaneous outstretching of her arms and a yawn that might swallow the world. There was the fragrant scent of something between chocolate-covered coffee beans and imported cookies centered with lemon filling, lined in a cursive coat of vanilla, her secret stash that might make even the well-fed feel if for a moment famished.

"I fell asleep! Sorry, my boy—life is long if you know how to live it. And in order to live it one must engage well with the craft of the nap! Part of its secret law is that it comes without warning. What, have I slept ten minutes? No—dear me! Two hours! Giuseppe, have you heard from mama or papa?"

"No, Nonna," said Giuseppe. "But Fr. Moritz is here."

"Well I'll be!"

Nonna patted Giuseppe on the head and turned down the wooden lever aside her chair.

"Tis I," announced Fr. Moritz, emerging with disheveled cape, strewn with a thousand microscopic crumbs. "Stopping by to see my favorite parishioner, the dear Nonna. I bring you a lucky blessed coin of St. John of the Cross, a second of St. John of God, and a pair of lottery tickets. I depart for the airport momentarily and thought I would stop by to say hello en route."

"Thank you, Father! Oh—wow, how beautiful! But the long number here," she rasped, "518–119-132-19. What is that?"

"Such was a strange whim, dear friend, involving numerical values and literature from many centuries ago."

"Like the Bible?" asked Giuseppe.

"Not quite so old as that. About as old as Christopher Columbus. Have you ever heard, my boy, of Erasmus of Rotterdam?"

"*Praise of Folly*," said the boy. "Mama used to read a picture version for me."

"I don't know what you are talking about," Nonna said, fishing her glasses out of apron pockets. "But I'll watch the numbers tonight." She cleared her throat. "When will you be back to visit, Father?"

"Soon, I hope," said the enormous priest, momentarily picking his nose. "But I am afraid the Society will get me excommunicated, so I cannot say in what fashion I'll return. They and their political partners have truly come to despise anyone who dares speak the truth any longer . . . firing men for being against abortion, refusing to say that all faiths are equally precise, and refusing to acknowledge homosexual union as marriages, just to begin. And you know, Nonna, I never even spoke publicly of these things. They are, rather, tenets of the faith, which lead anyone who degrades them into a dark place concerning just what dogma is and means. If it can change according to political trends, why bother with it at all? I have truly to come to hate so many of them, who started out living for the Bible, and ended up with intellectual ceilings no higher than corporate newspapers. There are a few good ones out of the batch, but it is too late now. The line has been crossed. Remember then that the kingdom of God is in you, and it is not a building or a man, neither architectures nor groups of men. It is the silence that becomes the music of solitude that is a refusal to justify evil. So I tell you, I am called to Rome, but I have managed to set aside some private funds over the years, and may very well change my name, grow a beard, dye my hair, and get a cheap room up north of here, then returning to live in Little Italy in, say, four years, when all the dust has settled."

"You might be able to confirm little Giuseppe," smiled Nonna. "I'll miss you, you know, but it is best that you go where your spirit can no longer be assaulted. Once-great groups of men devolve into mobs . . . and mobs are always composed of fierce animals."

"Nonna, a lady gave this to me; she is a student from Rodham acting in the play and I think she was doing a promotion with the lottery. So now you have two lottery tickets."

"Ah!" said Nonna joyously, "This is for the big one! Soon! Tonight!"

She reeled in Giuseppe and kissed him on the cheek.

For a time Fr. Moritz and Nonna discussed spiritual manners which, again, Giuseppe did his best to casually absorb. No doubt this neighborhood made him think for the first time of perhaps spinning fairy tales and little couplets himself, which was a new sensation; neither scholar nor poet in the family to speak of, the prospect of wearing a cloak, writing by feather and ink, and read big illuminated books that would one day be less the size of half his frame than something tangible, something real, to hold and cherish and live by.

Now the sunset was moving in earnest, and even the distant commotion of Arthur Avenue was winding down. An old suspendered man tossed bread crumb out all over some discarded tiles, and a swarm of pigeons moved in. The man yanked on a chain, and down came the awning—airbrushed by a collage of identical Italian flags—and bending, made a lightheaded groaning sound, striking a match and cradling it to his cigar, patting the debris off of his hands through a cloud of smoky debris.

XII.

Giuseppe genuflected, therein whispering, "Lord, thank you for making me back home safe today. Thank you for watching over me even when I was bad. I promise to never sneak out anywhere ever again. Please don't let my parents or Nonna find out." He opened one little eye and caught a glimpse of a framed, bespectacled pope making a stern two-fingered gesture at him. "And also I pray that daddy gets the job and mommy is happier and someday I have a little sister or brother to play with. That would be—"

The opening and closing of familiar, heavy car doors, followed by equally familiar voices—and behold!—mama and papa were laughing, with bags of goodies, and even holding hands!

The boy briskly genuflected, promised God he would soon, very soon, return to their private conversation, and for now leapt down from the old chair beside the windowsill, and washed his face, hands, though unsure how he would explain the bit of dirt here and there, considering mama might fly into a rage when she told him ten times before the day even got going that new clothes were not for playing in—and how could one get dirty, who had spend the afternoon with Nonna here, far from dirt and caca?

Giuseppe hid in the fresh julip-tinted bath towel he always used to dry his hands at Nonna's after dinner, therein folded up perfectly in a way by which were one to wash their hands after him and employ the same towel out of the four variegated hues and sizes available, one would believe it was fresh.

Then suddenly Nonna, Fr. Moritz were greeting Giuseppe's mama and papa in the living room; folding up the towel his efficient way, Giuseppe stayed back out into the living room.

"He wasn't too much of a pain, was he?"

"I never even know he's here; he's a little angel!"

"He knows his prayers, too," said Fr. Moritz, concealing what appeared a mammoth belch through some strange bodily motions and the extension of his pointer finger. "When they have the May Procession, I'll write in that Giuseppe is the one chosen out of the public school boys in Religion to carry the holy statue."

"But how, Father, when you'll be gone by then?" asked Giuseppe's father.

Giuseppe shuffled over to his mother and hugged her stockinged leg. She smilingly ruffled his hair.

"You see," belched Fr. Moritz, "They even let a man like me, an exile, put in some last requests." He removed a miniature decomposition book from a hidden pocket, and clicked on a pen. "I am noting here the request—met with Nonna, saw Giuseppe and parents," muttering fixedly while scribbling onward.

"Turn on the TV will you, the numbers are announced now."

Giuseppe's father rolled his eyes and turned on the TV.

"Did you get the job as the toll both collector, daddy?"

"That was last week, or no, two weeks ago," exhaled Giuseppe the Elder. He closed his dark eyes and scratched the edge of his right eyebrow, teeth halfway clenched with lips open, neck muscles springing outward. "Today was good though, I think they like me. It's at a grocery store in Jersey City. I'll start stocking shelves but there is a lot of room to move up. They also got a place in Redhook."

There was something so pathetic about the announcement it was both tragic and beautiful, contemporaneous and biblical. If it were not for Giuseppe's mother, perhaps the other members of his immediate and extended family would have helped Giuseppe the Elder along the way in life. But as it was, he lacked a college education, and he was furthermore an honest man. His condemnation in this life was less indicative of past abominations than it was a testament to the purity of his heart; even his fellow Roman Catholics despised him because he reminded them too much of Christ.

Naturally, Fr. Moritz loved him. But now even Fr. Moritz was out, along with the prospect of some hours helping keep the vast church tidy till some more stable work came along.

'If only I could share with papa the adventures of my day!' Giuseppe interiorly sniffled. Whatever joy he had heard out on the street seemed momentarily extinguished.

"Say," said Fr. Moritz, as the family sat down on the loveseat beside Nonna, "Do you think you could keep me in mind at the grocer, should you keep the job? If they need any other grocers: perhaps we could work there together until something else comes up. I'll grow a beard, wear glasses, and dye my hair."

"Of course, Father."

"Before I leave, let us raise a glass to Dietrich Bonhoeffer."

"Good evening, New York! Here are tonight's winning numbers—"

"I'll get dinner and drinks ready with my little helper—come, on Giuseppe—up! You must have had a busy day here!"

"O yes."

"Quiet!"

At the end of the inconsequential readings, the host came to the jackpot which had been running for thirty-nine weeks without winner, estimated at over ten million dollars.

"You are too young to chop garlic! Napkins—set down the napkins!"

"Five one eight; one, one nine; one three two; one, one nine. I repeat—"

Giuseppe heard a sound unlike any he had ever heard before in his life; and already halfway in the living room, he simply bolted around.

And there he saw Nonna, launched out of her chair and up, as if by some supernatural force, screaming in ecstasy; and Fr. Moritz's cheese went flying out of his pockets as his hitherto pocketed hands shot up to clutch his temples as he fell to his knees, singing, "Lord! LORD! LOOOOORD!"

Giuseppe's father scooped him up, dancing into the kitchen and with his astonished mother.

"I don't believe it, and it's not funny."

But then even she saw Nonna emerge from a downward, rosary-clutched position, bolting upward and screaming hallelujahs.

And she was dancing around the living room with Fr. Moritz, their collective minds on fire.

And Giuseppe looked out at Arthur Avenue, lit up, alive and well, and pinching himself thought again of the Trinity, the voices of the day, and the people who would soon know him and his family.

"We could do a lot of things with ten million bucks," said the exiled priest.

Nonna yanked up Giuseppe, covering him with kisses, and with him on her lap punched in the number up on the paused television screen, as his parents knocked back with the jolly priest.

And the bells of Our Lady of Mt. Carmel were ringing out.

www.ingramcontent.com/pod-product-compliance
Lightning Source LLC
Chambersburg PA
CBHW072008170626
46813CB00005B/2061